Blaze

Nina Levine

Blaze

Cover Design by LM Creations
   https://www.facebook.com/LMbookCreations
Formatting by Max Effect Author Services
   http://formaxeffect.com

Dedication

Blaze is dedicated to my readers.

It's dedicated to the readers who love J and
Madison as much as I do.

"Here's to those who inspire you and don't even know it."
-Anonymous

A Note About the Storm MC Series

Each book in this series continues on from the previous. While there won't be major cliffhangers in each book, there will be parts of the story that won't be resolved so please be aware of this.

★★★

In The Beginning

Madison
(Aged 22)

I FLOPPED DOWN ONTO THE COUCH IN THE CLUBHOUSE bar. It had been a long morning with my mother, helping her do some cleaning at the clubhouse. We'd finished up about half an hour ago and I was waiting for her to do a couple of other things before she could drive me home. My car was at the mechanics today being serviced so I was relying on her for a lift back there to collect it. I pulled my book out of my bag and flipped to the page I was up to. It was the latest Jackie Collins book and I needed to know what happened to the asshole who was cheating on his wife. Damn, nobody wrote a book as well as Jackie did.

I don't know how long I'd been engrossed in the book when I heard a voice say, "So, it's your birthday tomorrow. What are you doing to celebrate?"

I looked up to find J looking down at me. He'd just gotten back from a ride and was all sweaty but I didn't mind; the smell of sweat mixed with the sandalwood scent he wore kind of drove me wild. On days like today, when he looked rough and ready after a ride, it was hard being only friends with him. I wanted more. However, I valued our friendship of nearly six years and didn't want to risk losing it by taking a chance on something I knew wouldn't lead anywhere. J wasn't the kind of guy to settle down with anyone. He'd had a couple of girlfriends over the years but they never seemed to last long; six months was the longest I think I'd ever seen him with someone. Our friendship on the other hand, had lasted the distance.

He nudged my leg with his boot. "You going to answer me or are you going to keep daydreaming?"

"Shit, sorry," I muttered as I jumped up. Thank goodness he couldn't read my mind; that would have been awkward. "I'm going out to Hydes tonight, with some friends. Scott's going to be there; do you want to come too?" I tried to ignore my desperate desire for him to say yes. Actually, it would probably be better if he said no because if he did come, things could get messy if I threw myself at him after a couple of drinks.

He smiled. "Sure, count me in. I've got some things to do but I'll be there later on."

My heart skipped a beat and the butterflies in my stomach went into overdrive. "Great." Shit, was that the best I could do? Great? Lately, I was like a bloody school girl when I was around J; the things that came out of my mouth were embarrassing. Right now, he was so close to me that it was messing with my thought process.

He smirked and I watched as his eyes dropped to my chest that was covered by the tightest tank top known to man. It was a bloody hot day today so I was wearing very little clothing, and right about now, I was secretly thankful for that. I liked him looking at me this way. His eyes lingered on my chest for awhile before continuing their path down my body to my legs that were bare thanks to the short denim shorts I was wearing. The sensations this caused in me were like nothing I'd ever experienced. Sure, I'd had a number of boyfriends and wasn't a virgin anymore, but there was something about J; he made me feel things that both excited and terrified me.

His eyes finally found their way back to mine and he murmured, "Wouldn't miss it, sweetheart."

There was something in the way he spoke that caused me to stop and soak in his words. He hadn't said it in the way a friend would say it; there'd been more to his words than that. I tilted my head and gazed up at him. He was watching me closely; his eyes were focused solely on mine now, not on my body. They burned into mine with an intensity that thrilled me. The world around me stopped and my attention was completely on J in that moment. Finally, I said softly, "Good, I'm glad you can make it."

We stood staring at each other for a moment longer before my father interrupted us. "J, you got a minute?" he called out from the hallway.

J turned and nodded at him. "Be there in a minute," he said and then turned back to me.

"I'll see you tonight," he promised, and then left me to go find my dad.

I watched him go; still stunned at the turn that conversation had taken. And shit, now I had to rethink my whole outfit for tonight; if J was coming, I had to rethink everything.

★★★

Eight hours later, I was happily tipsy. Okay, maybe I was a little more than tipsy but I wasn't drunk. And J still hadn't turned up. I'd been waiting for him all night but when he still hadn't shown up an hour ago, I'd decided he wasn't coming and had thrown myself into having a good time with my friends who had come and forgetting him; forgetting my extreme disappointment that he'd not come.

I was stumbling out of the ladies room when a strong arm curled around my waist and held me up; held me close to him. "Babe, how much have you had to drink?" he breathed into my ear.

His breath on my skin sent shivers through me and I instinctually leaned into him; the need to get closer was overwhelming. "A little bit," I replied.

He chuckled. "Looks like a lot more than a little."

I shrugged. "I was waiting for you and you didn't come so I passed the time another way." Somewhere in the back of my fuzzy mind, I was kicking myself for admitting that to him.

He froze and turned me slightly so that we were facing each other, his hand still gripping my waist. "Fuck, Madison," he muttered, his eyes searching mine. "You want this as much as I do, don't you?"

Now I was really confused. "Want what?" I asked.

"Jesus, you've got to know by now that I want you in my bed. I didn't know how you felt; you've always given me mixed signals but now I can see that you want it too."

Shit, this was not good. I shook my head. "No, J. It's not a good idea. I just want to stay friends with you and that won't happen if I sleep with you."

"Don't bullshit me, babe. You want this. It's fucking written across your face." He moved his hand from my waist to my ass, gripping it and pulling me to him. Leaning his face closer to mine, he murmured, "Your pussy's wet for me, isn't it?"

I knew I was done for in that instant. My desire for him, mixed with the alcohol in my system, collided, and all rational thought flew out the window. Unable to hold it in, I moaned. J caught it and that was enough for him; his lips smashed down onto mine and we began the dance of lust that could only lead to one place. His hands were all over my ass and then one hand moved around to my breast. As his fingers brushed over my nipple, I moved my hands to his ass and pulled him into me. His cock was hard against me and it felt so damn good.

He ended our kiss and pulled away from me slightly. "Christ almighty, I need to get you out of here."

I nodded, and looked around for my friends. If we were leaving, I needed to say goodbye to them.

J grabbed my hand and started to walk towards the door to leave. I pulled on his hand to stop him and he turned to look at me. "What?" he asked, reluctantly stopping.

"I need to tell my friends that I'm leaving."

Frustration crossed his face. "Really?" he asked, impatiently. "Can't you just text them? Cause I've gotta tell you, my dick's been hard for you for a long fucking time and I don't want to waste time fucking about looking for your friends."

Whoa. He was bossy, and damn, it turned me on even more. But I wasn't the kind of person to ditch a friend on a night out without telling them I was safe. "No, I can't just text them. I've got to at least find Bec and tell her where I'm going."

He let go of my hand and ran his fingers through his hair. "Okay, but make it quick, babe. I'm not kidding when I say that I've never been this hard for any other woman."

I almost tripped over when he uttered those words. Confusion crowded my mind; how had I missed the fact that J wanted me as much as I wanted him? And just what did he want? One night? Or something more permanent? I realised that in that moment, I didn't care; I wanted tonight with him and tomorrow we could sort out the rest. I just hoped that with whatever happened, we would remain friends because I valued the friendship we'd built over the years; J meant more to me than most of my girlfriends and I didn't want to lose that. Friends could have sex. Couldn't they?

★★★

We pulled up outside his house and I got off his bike and stood silently watching him. I was nervous which was unlike me. It was disconcerting to have knots in my stomach and to feel speechless around him.

He stayed on his bike, slowly removed his helmet and looked at me. "What's wrong, babe?"

"What are we doing?" I asked softly, the passion I'd felt at the club had given way to nerves now.

He cocked his head to the side. "I thought we'd agreed on that already."

I nodded. "We had but -"

He cut me off, his voice laced with frustration, "But what, Madison? It's a no brainer for me. I want you and you want me. What's there to think about?"

"Everything. There's everything to think about. You're one of my best friends and I don't want to lose that."

"Why would we lose that?" The confusion was clear on his face.

I sighed; why did men have to be so clueless? "So we have sex tonight. What happens tomorrow? Will it be awkward between us or do you think we can just go back to being what we were before tonight?"

"Fuck. Why do chicks have to fucking over analyse shit? Why can't we just have tonight and go from there?"

He got off his bike and walked towards me but I took a step back. He'd annoyed me now with his attitude towards this. When I stepped back, he stopped and shook his head. "So that's it? You've changed your mind?"

"Well, I had hoped that we could discuss it a little more but you don't seem to want to do that."

"Babe, I seriously just want to get you inside and get your fucking clothes off. As far as I'm concerned that's all the discussion that we need to make this happen."

"Yeah, well I think that you and I are talking about two different things now, J. You seem to just want a quick fuck and I'm more interested to know what happens beyond that quick fuck." Disappointment settled in; I'd thought he wanted more but it looked like I was wrong. This was why you didn't contemplate having sex with your male friends.

His phone rang and he scowled. Answering it, he barked, "I'm in the middle of something. What's up?" His eyes did not leave mine.

I stood waiting for him to finish his conversation; the intensity of his glare stirring up the butterflies in my stomach. That glare was a mixture of heat, desire, frustration, annoyance and so much more. I felt the exact same things that he was projecting. However, in that moment, my annoyance at his attitude outweighed my desire to be with him.

He ended his call and put his phone back in his pocket. "I've got to be at the clubhouse in an hour. Are we going to do this or not?"

Un-fucking-believable. "I can't believe you just said that. No, we're not doing this," I snapped, and reached into my bag to get my phone out.

He stepped into my space and placed his hand over mine, stopping me. "I'm not sure what the fuck happened in your mind between the club and here, babe. Unfortunately, I don't have the time to fuck about so I'll just take you home, but this is a conversation that needs to be finished at some point."

I shook my head. "No, I'll find my own way home, and this is not a conversation that needs to be revisited. You've made your intentions pretty clear."

His nostrils flared and his breathing grew ragged. "I'm taking you home, Madison." He made his way back to his bike and tried to pass me the helmet. "Put this on and get on the bike."

My eyes widened. I wasn't used to J talking to me like this. Ignoring him, I scrolled through my phone looking for the phone number of my only friend who hadn't been out drinking with me tonight; hopefully she'd be able to come and pick me up. I finally found her number and hit dial, returning the glare that J was sending my way. She finally answered her call and agreed to come and get me.

J folded his arms across his chest and planted his feet wide. He was angry now and didn't hold back. "Why the fuck couldn't you just let me take you home?"

"Because you're being a prick and I don't want to be anywhere near you," I threw back.

"So now I've got to wait here until your friend arrives. Would have been a lot easier to do it my way."

"No-one's asking you to stay!"

"Jesus, Madison. As if I'd fucking leave you alone at this time of the night."

I was exasperated. On the one hand, I wanted to punch him, but on the other hand I wanted to rip his clothes off and screw him.

The next ten minutes were ten of the longest minutes in my life. We didn't speak while we waited for Sally to come and get me. Instead, J paced and threw me a foul look every now and then. I sank further into my disappointment. When she pulled up, I quickly got in her car without a backwards glance at J. I could feel his angry eyes on me though. I must have been out of my mind to think that he and I could take our friendship further.

★★★

I woke up on my birthday and felt like shit. Not only did I have a headache from the slight hangover I had, but I felt ill over what had happened with J last night. Luckily I hadn't planned anything special; it meant that I could pretty much just keep to myself. And so it was that I spent most of the day at home, reading and eating junk food. I wallowed in my heartbreak, because it was true, I was heartbroken that not only did I screw up a chance at a relationship with J but I'd probably screwed up our friendship too.

He never called or came by but at three o'clock that afternoon, I heard the rumble of a bike outside. Figuring it was Scott, I ignored it, stuck my headphones in and went back to my book. I didn't want to see anyone.

A couple of minutes later, my headphones were ripped out of my ears and J stood in my bedroom, staring down at me. I couldn't pick his mood. He seemed mildly annoyed but at the same time, he had a soft look in his eyes.

I moved off the bed so I was face to face with him. "What are you doing here, J?"

"Came to say happy birthday." His voice was soft. It did things to me and I mentally cursed him; it wasn't fair that he could make me feel this way when I was so upset with him.

"Thanks."

His eyes scanned my face. I wasn't sure what he was looking for but I figured he hadn't found it when he muttered, "Fuck. This isn't going to be easy, is it?"

Good God, he confused the shit out of me. "What isn't going to be easy?"

His chest rose and fell in a heavy movement. "Us."

"What, our friendship?" I really wished we were doing this on any other day than today. Today I wasn't feeling the best so I was struggling to keep up with him.

A look crossed his face and then he appeared to settle something in his mind. He grabbed my hand and began walking us out of the bedroom.

"Where are we going?" I asked while trying to slow him down by pulling back.

It was futile though; he just kept powering through the house and out the front door. He let go of my hand once we were outside so that he could lock the front door.

"Where did you get a key for my house?" I had no clue that he had that key.

"Scott gave it to me. We've both got one in case you ever needed us."

He said that like it was the most normal thing in the world. As far as I was concerned, it wasn't. "I want that key back. And Scott's too. You guys don't need to worry about me."

His amused eyes landed on mine and he shook his head. "Not going to happen, babe."

Before I could say anything else, he grabbed my hand again and directed us to his bike. He handed me a helmet and indicated for me to put it on.

Again, I argued. "Tell me where we're going."

"Got a place I want to show you." He pointed at the helmet and then the bike. "Put it on and get on the bike."

I assessed the situation and decided it was just going to be easier to do what he said so I did. Moments later his bike roared to life and we took off. I held onto him tightly and eventually relaxed. Having grown up around bikes my whole life, I loved being on the back of one. And being on the back of J's, with my arms wrapped around him, felt amazing. Exhilarating. It felt like I was home, and I had no idea where that thought came from, but it was what was swirling around my mind.

Just under an hour later, he pulled the bike off the road and killed the engine. We were at Mt Glorious. It was beautiful but I was curious as to why he'd brought me here. He led me along a path until we eventually came to a small clearing. I'd been to Mt Glorious before; it was a great ride on a bike. But I'd never been to this particular part of it. The view was stunning. We could see out across the valley and it was just beautiful. There was no-one else around and the sounds of any cars were muted by the bush. There really was only one word to describe what my senses were getting from all of this; peace. It was peaceful here and it calmed me.

J was watching me quietly while I took all of this in. Finally, I looked at him and asked, "Why are we here, J?"

He nodded slowly. "This is where I come when I need to clear the shit out of my head."

"Okay," I said, waiting for him to go on.

"I've been coming here a lot over the last six months."

I raised my eyebrows. "Had a lot of shit to clear out, I take it."

His mouth curved up slightly in a small grin. "Yeah, you could say that, babe."

"Okay, so tell me. What's this got to do with me?"

"Everything." He was watching me intently. It looked like he had a lot to say but he was holding back for some reason.

"Goodness, J. You need to get to the point. I don't have the patience today to -"

He cut me off. "This is where I decided to make you mine." His words were rough but tender if that was even possible.

Whoosh. The butterflies took hold of my stomach at those words. I was speechless.

He continued. "Been thinking about you for the past six months, Madison. Can't get you out of my fucking mind. So, I've been coming here to think. Last night, after I screwed the fuck up with you, I came here. And I decided you'd be mine before today was over."

He was so bossy. I'd never had a guy like J before, but standing there, listening to him claim me like a caveman, I knew that I was ruined for all men. J was going to ruin me and consume me, and I was going to let him.

I moved into him at the same time that he reached his hand out and wrapped it around my neck to pull me closer. Our lips found each other and he began to ruin me. Our bodies were pressed together, our hands were on each other and I came alive under his touch. Desire spread through me as I fought to get even closer to him, as I gave myself over to this kiss.

Eventually we pulled apart, but he kept a hold on me, keeping me close so that we were still touching. "Fuck, babe. Those lips of yours might be my fucking downfall."

I smiled up at him; at his words. And then my smile turned wicked. "I think there'll be other parts of me that might be your downfall."

His eyes widened and then he shook his head, and muttered, "You might be fucking right there."

"So, now that I'm yours, are you going to take me home and have your way with me? Because, even though this will always be known as our special place, I've got to admit, I don't really like to rough it."

He moved his mouth close to my ear, and murmured, "I'd love to fuck you here, babe. Out in the open; could be kinda hot. But I totally get that you're not a roughing it kind of chick. And I want you completely fucking relaxed when I finally get those panties off you and my cock into you."

Holy fuck, he had a dirty mouth. And I fucking loved it.

I grabbed his hand and started walking us towards his bike. When he slowed and pulled on my hand to slow me down, I turned and muttered, "Hurry up, J. You've got a promise to fulfill."

His face spread into a huge smile. "Just making sure this is what you want, sweetheart."

"Oh, so now, after you tell me how it's going to be and promise your cock to me, you decide to see what I want. Well, even though you've already decided for me, you can rest assured that I want this too. But what I really, really want right now is for you to take your dirty mouth home and show me just what you can do with it."

"Fuck me," he growled, and with that he grabbed my hand and took me home.

Prologue

September - Current Time
(Picks up where Storm finished, J has just returned)

Madison

"BABE, WHAT THE FUCK HAPPENED TO OUR BATHROOM?"

I looked up from the book I was reading to find J standing in the doorway of our bedroom with a perplexed look on his face.

"Huh?" I was engrossed in my book and had no idea what he was talking about.

"Madison, when I left two months ago the bathroom was white. Care to tell me why it now has different patches of colour on the wall?"

"Oh, that." I was still dividing my attention between my book and J; it was a damn good, sexy book and I was slightly annoyed that he'd interrupted me when I was just at a good part in the story.

"Yeah, that," he said, and the tone he took crawled across my skin. I quickly looked up at him; he was pissed. But I had to give him credit because he was containing it.

I turned my Kindle off and laid it on the bed before getting up and walking towards him. "I thought we could paint the bathroom and I was trying out different colours to see what they would look like. I didn't think you would mind," I said softly because I knew that J reacted favourably when I used my soft voice on him. I was trying to work out why he was mad about this; it was just paint for goodness sake.

Our eyes locked and we were both silent while he processed what I'd said. Finally, he blew out a breath and ran his fingers through his hair. "Sorry, babe. It's all good; I'm just on edge at the moment. I didn't mean to take it out on you," he apologised before pulling me close and wrapping his arms around me. When he pressed his lips gently to my head in a kiss, I melted a little into him and let my annoyance at him go.

We stayed like that for a moment and then I pulled away, and asked, "What's got you on edge?"

I watched his silent war as he fought his natural tendency to shut me out. He'd been back in Brisbane for a day and I'd sensed club problems already. J had spent the day taking care of club business and had come home in a subdued mood. The only time I'd seen him perk up was this afternoon when everyone had been giving Scott grief about trying to hook up with a guy that he thought was a woman. We'd been home for about four hours now and he hadn't even tried to have sex with me; instead he'd sat playing his X-box after dinner so I'd retreated to the bedroom with my book. I figured it might be a good idea to give him some space.

"We've got some staffing issues at Indigo," he said. I watched him closely and knew from the way his eyes avoided mine that there was something else bothering him.

"And?" I gently nudged him.

His eyes found mine again and I saw the shift in them as he finally decided to open up to me. I wasn't going to push him on this; I'd have been happy to let him slowly sink back into our relationship after his time away. But it seemed that J was ready to take us to a new level and I was happy about that.

"Marcus is being a prick. I know he's your dad, Madison, but he and I will never have a good relationship again."

"I don't care, J. I hate him for what he's done to our family and I don't want anything to do with him anymore. I told you that already."

"Yeah baby, but it's all still fresh for you. In time you'll move on from that but I don't think he and I ever will. He's changed in the last couple of months. I mean, he's always been an asshole but I at least had some respect for him. That's all gone now, especially after the way I saw him treating some of the boys today. He doesn't seem to have any respect for us anymore so why would we give that to him? He's my President and I'll do what he says as far as the club's concerned but outside of that, I don't want anything to do with him."

I took in the tenseness of his jaw and the worry lines creasing his face, and ached to take all of that away for him. Reaching my hand up to his cheek, I softly ran my thumb across it. "J, you've been back for twenty-four hours and already you're worrying about stuff that you don't need to be worrying about. Your relationship with my father is exactly that; yours. I don't want you to factor me into that at all. In fact, forget he's my father because I sure as hell want to."

He reached his hand up and placed it over mine, stilling me. "Babe, it's all well and good to say that now but what's to say in six months or sooner, you patch things up with him. What then? I don't want him coming between us and I worry that he will."

Shaking my head, I tried to ease his mind. "No, I won't let that happen. I promise. We've worked too damn hard to get us back on track; I'm not going to let anything or anyone mess it up again."

J still didn't look convinced. I needed him to be but I had no idea how to do that so I resorted, for now, to the one thing that always brought us closer together. I moved into his space, pushing my body as close to his as I could get. The feel of him against me caused me to moan; we'd been apart for too long and I craved his touch like never before.

"Fuck, babe," he growled, and circled my waist with his arm, letting his hand rest on my ass. Our eyes locked and in that moment all outside issues took a back seat as we came together. He lowered his lips to mine and kissed me. I was surprised at the gentleness of it; J and I didn't do gentle very often. This kiss enveloped me though, with its tenderness; it joined us and connected us in a way that we desperately needed to be connected after months apart, and especially with all the problems surrounding us and my family.

I moved my hands to the bottom of his shirt and lifted it over his head. Dropping it to the ground, I ran my gaze over his chest. My stomach was full of butterflies and my heart rate was picking up; J turned me on more than any other man I'd ever been with. He'd packed more muscle on while he was away even though I would have sworn it wasn't possible to fit anymore on him.

He cut into my thoughts, "Baby, the way you're looking at me is making me so fucking hard. I like your eyes on me but I'd fucking kill to have your mouth on me."

I looked him in the eyes for a long moment before moving my mouth to his chest. My teeth gently grazed his nipple before I licked and sucked him. I then repeated this on his other nipple, teasing him because I knew that this wouldn't have been what he meant when he said he wanted my mouth on him. Once I was finished, I eyed him and murmured, "Is that where you wanted my mouth??"

He smirked before grabbing my chin in his hand. Rubbing his thumb over my lips, he muttered, "This mouth was made for my cock, sweetheart, and you damn well know it."

Smiling, I said, "I know, but it's so much fun to play with you first."

He raised an eyebrow. "So, we're finished playing now?"

As he continued to rub his thumb back and forth over my lips, I moved my hands down to his jeans and popped the button. I unzipped them, and let his cock free, catching it in my hand. "Yeah baby, we're finished playing now."

His reaction was fast. He roughly pulled me to him, one hand sliding around to grip my ass, and the other hand gripping the back of my neck to steady me. "Good, because I've changed my mind. I don't want your mouth on me anymore, I need to sink my dick as far in you as I can; need that sweet pussy of yours around me."

J's dirty words never failed to get me wet; I was so ready for him. "Baby, I've missed your dirty mouth the last few months," I whispered in his ear as he nuzzled my neck and kissed me.

"You've no fucking idea, sweetheart," he growled, "After you have my cock, I'm going to treat you to my mouth. And I promise you, no fucker will ever separate us again."

He scooped me up and carried me to the bed. His face had that intense look that I loved. It meant business; it meant that he was about to fuck me hard, just the way I liked it. He laid me down on the bed and I watched as he removed his jeans; there was nothing under them so he was now naked for me and what a glorious sight that was. I drank him in. J was only improving with age as far as I was concerned, and for a man that was pretty damn perfect to start with, that meant he was off the charts magnificent now. My gaze was drawn to a new tattoo on his chest; one I hadn't noticed since he'd been back. I sat up and traced it with my fingers. It was a circle but the line of the circle was broken up by numbers at two different sections, and the circle also wasn't complete. There was a swirly letter M in the centre of the circle.

"What does this tat mean?" I asked him, breaking into our heated moment.

He looked down at his chest and reached for my hand. Then he looked back at me; love shining out of his eyes. Letting go of my hand, he pointed at one of the numbers. "This is the date we first got together, your birthday years ago." He then pointed at the other number. "And this is the date we got back together this time."

"Why isn't the circle joined at the ends?" I asked.

"Because I need the date of our wedding. That will go in that gap and then the circle will be complete," he murmured without taking his eyes off mine.

Holy shit. In that moment, I realised just how much my man loved me. I reached my hand up and curled it around his neck, and pulled his lips to mine. We joined in a kiss that reached right down into my soul. My heart was completely his. Our lives would forever be entwined because I was never letting him go again.

J moved onto the bed and gently pushed me onto my back while continuing our kiss. His hands moved to my shirt and he pushed it up and over my head. We broke apart momentarily but hungrily found each other's lips again as soon as he had my shirt off. I moaned when his fingers slid into my panties and found my clit.

When his finger entered me, he groaned and broke our kiss. "Fuck, babe. You're ready to go, aren't you?" He was staring down at me through lust filled eyes; eyes that I could get lost in for days at a time.

I nodded. Pushing my body towards him at the same time that he thrust his finger back inside me caused him to go deep, and it felt so fucking good that I jerked in pleasure. Heat flashed across his face and he pulled out of me and ripped my panties off.

"Bra, babe. Get it off," he commanded forcefully.

Who was I to argue? I did as he said and he moved over me so we were skin to skin. His cock was hard against me; teasing me. I'd gone without him for months and I felt like a horny teenager who couldn't get enough. I needed him now; all of him, in every way I could have him.

He held himself over me and directed his cock to my entrance. I was wet and more than ready and he wasn't in the mood to fuck around. He thrust straight in, all the way, on a groan.

"Fuck, Madison. Never again ... never fucking again," he grunted as he pulled back out and thrust hard again.

I wrapped my legs and arms around him, and held on for dear

life as he fucked me. J was a man on a mission and I, for one, was not complaining. I squeezed my eyes shut and let the feelings overtake me completely.

"Babe, eyes. Need your fucking eyes," he growled.

I did as he said and opened them. What I found nearly made me come right then and there. He was fucking me hard but his gaze was full of love. It told me that I was unequivocally his.

I gripped on to him harder and tightened the hold my legs had on him in an effort to get as close to him as I could. There was a burning desire inside me to be joined to him in every possible way; my love for him had only grown while he'd been away.

As he continued to thrust in and out, I moved my hips to meet his thrusts and I knew I was getting close. "J, I'm going to come," I panted, knowing that he liked for me to wait for him. Tonight, however, I knew there was no way I could make it. He'd gotten me here fast.

He didn't answer me; simply nodded in his frantic rush to get himself off. This hadn't been about me, this fuck. No, this had been all for him and he was blindly pursuing his release.

I lasted another minute or so and then I lost control of my body to the pleasure. My head rolled back and I shut my eyes again as it took over. I came on a scream and everything around me blurred as I let it take over. J was lost to me in that moment; I knew he was still pounding into me but the intense bliss I was feeling was all I could focus on.

It wasn't until I heard him roar, "Fuck," that I scrambled to get my bearings again. He came with one last thrust and then collapsed on top of me, his face buried in my neck. I wrapped my arms tighter around him and kissed his neck. We stayed like that for awhile. I could have stayed there for hours but eventually he lifted his head and looked at me. "Christ, woman. I don't think I've ever come so hard in my life."

"Never again, right?"

He looked confused. "What?"

"Never again will you leave me for that long."

Pushing up off me, he nodded. "Never."

"Good, because if you do, I might just turn into queen bitch from hell."

He raised an eyebrow and smirked at me.

"What?" I playfully smacked him on the arm and pushed him off me.

He landed on his back, grinning like an idiot and then rolled onto his side, resting himself on his elbow. Reaching his spare hand out to rest on my stomach, he asked, "Just what would that entail? You being queen bitch, I mean."

I pouted, playing along; playful J was one of my favourites. "Well, I would withhold sexual favours for sure -"

He starting laughing and cut me off. "There's no fucking way you would ever be able to last the distance so if that's your sole method of driving me crazy you'd better rethink your plan."

"Are you saying that I couldn't go without sex?"

"Baby, you were fucking built for sex. I'd give you a day but that'd be it."

"I lasted two months!"

"That's because you didn't have my cock in the same room as you. Your pussy has a fucking tracking device for my dick built into it, I am sure of it."

Shit, he had me at that. I poked my tongue at him and rolled off the bed. "You're right, I can't turn you away. But trust me, if need be, I can be queen bitch," I said as I walked towards the bathroom.

"I have no fucking doubt, sweetheart," he muttered, but I could hear the playful tone in his voice.

Ten minutes later, I was clean after a shower, and exited the bathroom to find J passed out on the bed. It was so unlike him to do that; he must have been exhausted. I threw my t-shirt back on and headed out to the kitchen to get a drink. My phone was on the kitchen counter and the flashing light to indicate I'd received a text caught my eye. I smiled when I saw it was from Serena.

SERENA: Good to have biker boy home?

ME: Yeah but I think I killed him with the sex...

SERENA: That's my girl.

ME: You getting any, babe?

SERENA: Ha! Next question.

ME: I miss you...

SERENA: Well you did move the fuck away...

ME: Yeah...I did...

SERENA: Ok, ok...I admit it, I'd move for a hot ass like that too.

ME: BAM! Knew you'd admit it eventually.

SERENA: We will never talk of this again. I'm still pissed that I've lost my best friend.

ME: Talk of what?

SERENA: That's why I love you.

ME: Goodnight, honey.

SERENA: Night. Talk tomorrow.

Serena always brought a smile to my face; every woman should have a best friend like her.   We'd spent some time together last month in Coffs when I visited her and Blake but I wasn't sure when we'd see each other again. Maybe one day I'd convince her to move to Brisbane.

I switched off the lights and made my way back to the bedroom where J was fast asleep. Lingering in the doorway for a moment, I thought about our earlier conversation. J seemed concerned about my father and how he might come between us. I decided in that moment to do everything in my power to make sure that didn't happen. My relationship with my dad had often been a hard one over the years, and now that the truth had come out about his secret family and the way he treated Mum, I truly wanted very little to do with him. J really was the most important person in my life and I resolved to show him that.

Chapter One

2 months later
November

Jason

I CHECKED THE TIME.

Again.

Fuck.

I wanted to go home, wanted to be with Madison more than any-fucking-thing in the world, but I couldn't make myself do it. Everything had changed; I had changed. And I didn't know if she could accept these changes. And the not fucking knowing was driving me insane. It was driving me to do things I never did. Like not chasing her pussy like I fucking wanted to.

Shit.

I craved her pussy like a man fucking possessed. Craved those eyes of her on me. Craved those lips of her; wrapped around my dick and every-fucking-where else on me. And yet, here I was, at a fuck-ing strip club, at eight o'clock at night when I should have been at home with her.

I reached for my drink and swung my eyes to Scott as he came towards me. I nodded at him and then drained my glass.

His face creased with concern as he pulled up a seat next to me. "You alright, brother?"

There were no secrets between us, not even where his sister was concerned. I shook my head. "No."

"What the fuck's wrong?"

"Marcus. That's what the fuck is wrong."

"Christ. What did he do now?"

I stood up. "Need another drink to do this. You want one?"

He nodded yes and I headed to the bar to get them. When I came back with the drinks, he took his beer from me and threw half of it back fast.

"Figured this is going to hurt," he muttered.

"Yeah, brother. You could say that," I agreed and followed suit. The bourbon burned on the way down, just the way I liked it. I slowly placed the glass on the table between us and then started talking. "Marcus is a cunt. Sent me into some situations when I was away that caused me to do things I never fucking thought I'd do."

"And?"

"And now I don't know how to live with some of that. And I sure as hell don't know how to live with him in my life. And to top that the fuck off, I want to marry his daughter." I stopped and reached for my drink again, draining it faster than the last one. Eyeing him, my words sliced through the air, "You tell me how the fuck I do that. How do I love a woman whose father I want to take a fucking knife to and gut like the fucking animal he is?"

Scott quickly reached for his beer and downed it. "Christ, J. What the fuck did he make you do?"

This was about to hurt but it couldn't be avoided. "Your father is a master manipulator; more devious than I ever gave him credit for. I'm sure he has an agenda that neither of us are going to like." I paused and took a deep breath. "Marcus sent me to the Adelaide chapter, wanted me to deal with a suspected paedophile in the club. I found the fucker alright and confirmed the dirty shit he was up to. What Marcus failed to mention was that there was a ring of them in the town and that he already knew they existed. He also failed to mention that the asshole was the fucking VP of the club and that he was standing in the way of a club deal to move some coke."

"How long had he known they existed?"

Yeah, Scott was a smart guy. He could already see where this was going. "For over a fucking year."

His face constricted in anger as he connected the dots. "That motherfucker."

I nodded but didn't say anything else.

We sat with our fury for awhile before he asked, "He wanted you to take out the VP for him so they could move the coke deal through?"

"Yes."

"And he played on what happened to your cousin and your hatred of paedophiles." It wasn't a question; he knew. And it would only increase his hatred of his father once he'd put it all together.

"Yeah, brother."

"What did you do?" He said this as he motioned for more drinks to be brought to us. Thank fuck we owned this club; we'd need a lot more alcohol to get through this.

"I fucking played right into Marcus's hands. And, even though I don't regret what I did, I fucking hate that I walked into his trap."

"Fuck, J, get to the point. I'm not used to you being so god damned reflective."

The rage I'd been holding in for a long time reared it's ugly head and threatened to explode out of me but I kept it in check. Just. Scott hadn't done anything to deserve it. No, it could fester for awhile longer until I decided to unleash it on the one person who did fucking deserve it. After sculling the drink we'd just had brought over, I gave him what he'd asked for. "I walked into the worst fucking situation you could imagine; something I'll never wipe from my mind." My heart was beating wildly in my chest as the sick images flashed through my head. My mouth went dry and I fought the rising bile. "I lost it, brother. I used my bare hands to kill the two assholes in that room and then I found the VP who was the fucking ringleader and I dragged his death out so that he experienced pain like he'd never fucking dreamt of." I eyed the waitress and lifted my chin at her while holding up two fingers to indicate I needed two drinks. Scott did the same.

He took a moment; letting it sink in. "So, you're telling me that Marcus knew this was going on but he held off on dealing with it until it suited his fucking purpose? And he used you because he fucking knew you'd do exactly what he wanted due to your cousin being abused as a kid?" His anger was building.

"Yeah brother, that's what I'm telling you."

"Fuck."

I tossed back another drink and leant forward towards him. "I'm also telling you that Marcus took great fucking delight in thanking me for doing it. He's a sick fuck on top of everything else." My hard eyes penetrated his. "Now, you tell me just how the fuck I can be with Madison knowing that she would be fucking gutted to know this about her father, and knowing that she doesn't want secrets between us." I drank the other drink sitting in front of me.

Scott watched me and shook his head. "Got no fucking idea."

"Exactly."

I stood. It was way past the time to go home. My cock wanted Madison but the rest of me hoped like hell that she was asleep. I didn't want to confront any of this yet.

As I walked away from Scott, he called out, "What's Marcus's agenda?"

I stopped and turned back to him. "Don't know, brother. But it's gonna hurt, you can fucking bet on it."

"Fuck!" Scott roared.

I left him there. Marcus was successfully fucking with all of us but I felt for his kids the most. As much as I felt fucked over by him, they'd had to deal with the discovery that their father was far from the man they thought they loved. And that cut deep; I knew from personal experience. It laid scars on your soul that you never even knew existed; scars that hurt for years to come as you found them.

Chapter Two

Madison

MY ALARM WOKE ME AT SEVEN AND WHEN I REACHED FOR J, I was disappointed to find his side of the bed empty. An uneasy feeling hit my gut. J loved morning sex but we hadn't had it for a few weeks now. Add to that the fact we were only having sex every few days now and I was slightly worried. We'd always been a couple who had sex every day, often more than once.

I dragged myself out of bed and went in search of him. He was nowhere to be found. Instead, I found a scribbled note telling me he'd had to go in early to take care of some stuff with Griff. I sat down at the table for a moment, reading his note and trying to process the fact that he hadn't woken me up to at least say goodbye. Deciding I needed another opinion on this I rang Blake.

"Don't read too much into it, baby doll. Men aren't as fucking complicated as women like to make them out to be," Blake advised me a couple of minutes later.

Sighing, I said, "Really? Because he does my head in some days so if that's not complicated, I don't know what is."

"No, that's probably just you making shit up in your head."

If he'd been standing in front of me, I would have smacked him. "You men always stick together!"

He chuckled. "I'm not saying this for J's sake. I'm saying it for yours. You've decided to be with him, and as much as that concerns me sometimes, I'll always support your choices. If you want to make it work this time, you need to figure him out and stop overthinking everything."

"I don't think I'll ever figure him out completely but I'm working on not reacting to everything so quickly. I know that's one of my biggest problems."

I could sense his smile on the other end of the line when he said, "J's a lucky man. Now, I have to go because I've got customers to get to. But, you need to talk to him and find out what's going on; chances are it's not what you've been thinking. I'll try to call you tomorrow but I may run out of time. Love you."

"I love you more, Blake Stone," I replied and we hung up. Thank God I had Blake in my life; his advice about men was invaluable some days.

★★★

That afternoon, I ducked into the clubhouse on my way home from work to drop off some paperwork for Mum. I'd had a long day at work and was anxious to get in and out quickly to avoid running into my father. I also really just wasn't in the mood to talk to anyone. Of course, good intentions never go to plan; I ran into Nash on my way in.

"Whoa, sweet thing. Hold up," Nash said as he placed both hands on my upper arms and stopped me.

"Hey, Nash," I responded, trying to keep my focus on him rather than on the thoughts that were swirling around in my head.

He kept his hands on my arms and his eyes bore down into mine. "What's wrong, Madison?" I could hear the concern in his voice and it touched me. For all his cockiness and dirty talk, Nash was a sweetheart. We'd grown closer over the last couple of months and I'd come to rely on him to vent my frustrations to. He was also good to get a guy's perspective on stuff when I was mad at J.

"I just want to drop this paperwork off for Mum and then get out of here," I answered him, doing my best to avoid his questioning gaze. Nash could read people really well and tonight I didn't want to be read. I just wanted to get home.

He shook his head, and grabbed my hand. "Nope, not good enough, darlin'. You're coming with me and you're going to talk."

Shit.

He led me out of the hallway and into the bar area where we could be alone.

"Nash, I really don't have time for this today," I complained as he forced me onto a barstool.

"I've learnt that we need to make time for this type of shit, otherwise people like us fall back into old habits," he replied, thoughtful eyes scanning mine. "And that's a place you don't want to go."

"You're being dramatic. I'm not about to rush out and have a bloody drink over this."

"No, but if you keep it locked up it will fester. Now, tell me what's wrong."

I blew out a long breath, and realising that he wasn't going to let this go, I started talking. "It's J. He's not himself and I'm not sure how to handle it."

"What do you mean, not himself?"

I felt guilty talking to Nash about this. J wasn't a huge fan of Nash's so I didn't feel it was right to talk about our problems with him. In the past, I hadn't shared specific problems with Nash; I'd just talked in general terms about men.

Nash was a perceptive man and picked up on my hesitation. "He's not giving you the cock you need?"

"God, Nash." I shook my head at his phrasing.

"What? I'm wrong?"

Again, I hesitated. J would be livid if he knew I was having this conversation.

"So, I'm right. What's his problem? If you were my woman, you'd never go without my cock, and you'd be fucking assured that it'd be the best damn sex you'd ever had."

I had to smile at his words this time; so confident and self assured. I liked that in a man. "Tell me, if you did have a woman, what would cause you to stop putting out?"

He chuckled. "I'll answer that but let's be clear, that would never fucking happen. The only thing that would stop me would be if the connection was broken."

I sat there stunned. Nash, flirty Nash who had sworn off relationships, had probably just hit the nail on the head and I would never have expected that from him. I leaned closer to him and half whispered, "What else do you have tucked away in your heart that you're hiding from the world?"

He didn't even flinch. Instead, he leaned even closer to me so that our faces were now inches apart, and whispered back, "Everything. There's no need to spread that shit around." He pulled back away and continued, his voice louder now, "But you, sweet thing, have a fucking way of getting in there, so take what I tell you and use it to fix your shit. One of us should benefit from my demons."

Warmth spread through me. This was a rare glimpse into Nash. He kept himself hidden and locked away; I'd always known that, but slowly he was revealing himself to me. I wondered how long it would take to drag the demons from his soul. I touched his arm lightly and smiled at him. "I wish you'd show your real self to more people. There's a beautiful soul in there, I can tell. Thank you for that."

He stood up abruptly, his face darkening. "This is the real me, babe. Don't fucking mistake me; I'm the bastard you've always known."

I looked up at him and shook my head. "No, I don't believe

that."

"Believe what you want, Madison, but don't delude yourself. I am who I am," he muttered before turning to leave. He took a couple of steps and then turned back to me to add, "Like your new hair by the way; suits you."

I gave him a huge smile. I'd added some highlights to my hair and had it layered two days ago and J hadn't noticed. That had hurt. "Thanks, Nash," I said.

He nodded and then he left me to sit and mull over everything he'd said. I must have sat there for ten minutes or so thinking about it before coming to the conclusion that Nash was right; my connection with J was off. Now I just had to work out if it was because of life getting in the way or if there was something deeper that needed fixing.

Chapter Three

Madison

"WE'RE GOING OUT NEXT FRIDAY, RIGHT? GIRLS NIGHT."
I was at Harlow's cafe and said this to her as she passed me my
morning coffee.

She grinned at me. "Hell, yeah."

I drank some of my coffee before confiding, "Thank God. You
have no idea how much I need a girl's night."

"What's wrong, honey?"

I didn't hold back; I'd been keeping this bottled up for too long
and needed to talk to her about it. "It's J. He's pulling away from me
and our sex life has gone to shit."

"Wow, really? You and J having problems in the bedroom;
never thought that day would come."

"I know!" I blurted out. "But we are, and I hate it. I need to fix
it so you have to tell me how."

She laughed. "Why me? I'm far from a sex therapist. Trust me,
I've had a lot of bad sex in my life."

I shook my head. "No, our problems aren't that the sex is bad,
because it's not. We have great sex, awesome fucking sex, and that's

why I need more. I need to know how to fix our connection and you're good at working out people, so you need to work out what J's problem is."

"I still hardly know J. He's distant and I can't get a handle on him." She had that thoughtful Harlow look in her eye so I knew she was thinking about it now. That was good; I had faith that she could help me crack this.

"Yeah, he's slowly becoming more and more distant," I agreed.

"You know, whenever your Dad is around or the conversation involves him, J retreats into his moody, pissed off self. It's like he doesn't want a bar of Marcus."

"He doesn't. He's told me that."

She cocked her head to the side. "Why? I mean, apart from the obvious, is there something else going on with those two?"

I thought about it for a moment. "I just thought it was because of their fight. Do you think something else has happened between them?"

"Maybe. You should ask him, suss out whether that could be it."

Smiling, I said, "Thank you. I knew you would be able to help."

"Anytime." She looked at the clock. "Now, I hate to tell you to leave, but if you don't go soon, you're going to be late for work."

I quickly finished off my coffee and stood up to leave. "You've always got my back, haven't you?" I leant across the counter and gave her a quick kiss on the cheek. "Love you."

★★★

I was still turning this over in my head that night as I put J's dinner in the oven. It was just after nine pm and he wasn't home from work yet. He'd been coming home later and later, and I had no idea what time to expect him. But I'd decided to try to talk to him tonight; to find out what was bothering him.

I was startled out of my thoughts when I heard a crash at the front door. "J, is that you?" I yelled out.

"Yeah," he called back; it didn't sound like he was in a good mood.

A moment later he appeared in the kitchen and dumped a cat cage on the floor. Straightening, he muttered, "Scott better fucking appreciate this."

I took one look at Monty and quickly let him out of the cage. "Shit, I forgot to tell you that I'd agreed to have him this weekend. Sorry, baby." Scott was taking Harlow away for the weekend and now that Monty pretty much lived at his house, he'd asked me to look after him. J hated cats; that's why I'd failed to mention it to him.

He was clearly annoyed. "The things you'd do for Scott and the things I'd fucking do for you."

His words were just what I needed to hear. With all the thinking I'd been doing about him and our relationship today, it was a relief to know that he felt that way. I smiled at him, and said, "Thank you."

He pulled me to him and roughly kissed me before saying, "I'm gonna hit the shower and then probably go to bed. It's been a long day and I'm wiped."

Disappointment flooded me and I felt like I had whiplash from my emotions. One minute, happy with him and the next upset. He'd come home late, he hadn't eaten the dinner I'd cooked for him and now he was just going to go to bed without spending any time with me. Before I could say anything, he was gone.

And I hadn't gotten the chance to talk to him about us.

And he still hadn't noticed my hair.

★★★

The next morning, J was in the shower when I woke up. I got out of bed and headed into the kitchen to get the coffee going. Determination to talk to him took over, and seems as though it was the weekend now, we would have plenty of time to talk.

He joined me ten minutes later, and the first thing I noticed was that he looked exhausted. Then I noticed that he wasn't dressed in his casual weekend stuff, but rather he looked like he was heading to the clubhouse.

"Are you going out?" I asked.

He avoided my gaze, and busied himself with making breakfast. "Yeah," was all he said.

"It's Saturday, J. I thought we could do something together today. Thought we could talk about what's going on between us." I held my breath and waited for his response.

He stilled, but didn't look at me. Eventually, he did turn around. "I've got stuff to do at the clubhouse."

I saw the guilt on his face. There was definitely something going on; something he didn't want to talk about. I decided to push the point. "That's okay, we can talk when you get home."

He frowned, but then nodded. "Yeah," he said, quietly, and then turned back to finish getting his breakfast.

I watched him for another minute or so. My appetite had vanished and I felt an urgent need to be on my own, away from J, so I grabbed my coffee and took it into the bedroom. I felt his eyes on me as I left but he never said a word so I didn't stop.

Tonight, we would talk.

Which meant that I would spend the day psyching myself up for it.

★★★

At nine o'clock that night, I reached into the oven and pulled the cupcake tray out. "Son of a bitch," I yelled out as the tray burnt my finger. I dropped it onto the bench and slammed the oven shut. Turning the tap on, I ran the cold water over the burn on my finger. "Fucking asshole," I muttered.

I was startled by a deep rumble. "Who's the asshole?"

J.

I didn't turn to look at him, just kept running the water over my finger and staring at the sink. "You. You're the asshole."

He didn't say anything but I could hear his heavy breathing. And then I couldn't. I turned my head to find him gone.

What the fuck?

What the fucking fuck?

I flicked the tap off and stalked out of the kitchen in search of him.

He was in the bathroom and it looked like he was about to take a shower. This meant that he planned on going to bed because J always showered before bed. And I just knew in my heart and my gut that he'd had no intention of having that talk with me.

His eyes avoided me as I stood watching him take his shirt off. He undid his belt and unbuttoned his jeans. My body was tingling with anger and lust. I wanted him but the heavy disappointment that was running through me had to be dealt with first.

Before he could remove his jeans, I reached out and laid my hand on his. "Stop," I breathed into the tense air that surrounded us.

His hand stilled and he slowly lifted his head to look at me. His eyes held something there that I never thought I'd ever see, and I flinched and pulled my hand away from his. *He didn't want me here.*

We stood watching each other. Warily. I hated it; this feeling of not knowing what he was thinking. Of knowing that he would rather I not be here with him.

Finally, I spoke. "Where have you been?" *Why don't you want me?*

"At the club." The smell of bourbon permeated the room. He'd been drinking; J hardly ever drank.

"You've been drinking."

"Christ, Madison. Can we not get into this right now?"

"Let me guess, it's been a long day and you're wiped." I threw his words from last night back at him.

He shoved his hand through his hair and blew out a long

breath. "Yeah, it has."

I don't know what I expected him to say but it hadn't been that. A little more fight perhaps. After all, it was what we did best. But this, this resignation that bled from him was the last thing I'd expected. There was something going on with J that he wasn't telling me. And as a woman, I struggled not to jump to conclusions. I couldn't stop myself though; it's what women did best. Random thoughts assaulted my mind; throwing various scenarios at me. In the space of a couple of minutes I must have conjured up at least five different theories as to why he was acting this way. And I knew that it was going to drive me insane. And I hated that too.

Deciding the best course of action was to not provoke him, I nodded. "Okay." I took one last look at him, and noting that the look in his eyes hadn't changed, I left him and made my way back to the kitchen.

I stood at the bench, staring at the mess I'd created. I lost track of how long I stood there but I guessed it must have been at least twenty minutes. The shower wasn't running anymore, however J never came back to the kitchen. I knew he wouldn't. He would either be asleep or pretending to be by the time I went to bed. My heart was hurting; I just wanted the J who had gone away four months ago back, not the J who had taken his place.

★★★

Sunday flew by without us talking about our problems. J was called out to deal with some Storm issues so I was once again left alone. Then Monday rolled around and I woke to discover J already gone again. I forced myself out of bed and into the shower so I could get ready for work. Disappointment sat heavy in my chest.

The morning passed by in a blur; shower, coffee, drive to work and then before I knew it, it was five o'clock and time to go home. As I put the keys in the ignition of my car, I realised that I didn't want to go home. Didn't want to see that look in J's eyes again.

Shit.

I sat there for a long time, thinking. And then I knew where I needed to be. I started the car and drove on autopilot to the place that had saved my soul already this year. It was my safe place and I needed it now.

Forty minutes later, I stood and said, "Hi, my name is Madison and I'm an alcoholic."

Tonight's meeting lasted just over an hour and I didn't hang around afterwards. I'd gotten what I'd needed and felt a little stronger, a little more able to attempt to talk to J tonight. My day had been spent going over and over it in my mind and I knew that I needed to sort it out as soon as possible. For my sanity if nothing else.

As I pulled into our driveway, I noted that he was home; his Jeep was parked in his side of the carport. Knots formed in my stomach and I was tempted to hit reverse and leave.

"Put your fucking big girl panties on," I chastised myself and put the car in park instead. I quickly grabbed my bag and got out of the car before I changed my mind.

As I reached to open the front door, J flung it open from the inside, his eyes wild. "Where have you been? I've been fucking worried about you."

My anger flared and I couldn't hold it in any longer. I shoved past him and stormed inside, throwing my bag on the bench when I hit the kitchen. He'd followed me and I spun around to glare at him. "You're seriously kidding me! I've spent the last God-knows-how-many nights waiting for you to come home with no word from you as to when that would be. You don't get to fucking yell at me for the same thing, J!"

"So this is tit for tat, is it?"

"No! I was just pointing out the obvious."

"It's not the obvious, Madison. You knew I was at work; I had no clue where you were seems as though you left work nearly three hours ago. A simple phone call would have been enough."

I stared at him incredulously. "I didn't know you were at work!" I yelled at him.

"Fuck, babe. It wouldn't have been hard to figure it out. Where the fuck else would I be?"

"I don't know, J. You tell me."

He stopped and stared at me, his eyes blinking as he tried to process a veiled accusation that I didn't actually mean. It had just come out of my mouth in a heated moment in which I wasn't thinking straight. Damn those scenarios I'd mentally flicked through last night; they were putting ideas in my head.

"I'm going to forget you said that," he said in a low, angry voice.

Trying to calm down, I took a couple of deep breaths. It didn't really work though; the adrenaline was coursing through me and I was at the point where I needed answers. I needed to know what was going on in his head. "J, where are you?"

He looked confused. "What?"

I shook my head; more at myself than him. That question hadn't come out right. I tried again. "I mean, there's something going on in your head and you're withdrawing from me. I need to know where your head's at." I took another deep breath before adding the one thing I didn't want to say. "If you don't want to be with me, you need to tell me."

His response was swift. He stepped forward and wrapped his arms around me, pulling me to him roughly. His lips brushed across the top of my forehead. I sank into him. This was what I needed; this closeness. J and I connected when we touched. It was like air to us; without it we stumbled.

"I fucking love you so don't ever confuse my distance for a lack of desire or commitment. I've just had some club shit to deal with, babe."

My hands ran over his back muscles. He was tense; rock hard. I wanted him to let me in. But he seemed to still be working out how to do that. So, I decided to give him that; to give him the time to figure his shit out. I had his words of commitment for now and that would have to be enough until he could give me more.

I pulled away. "I love you too," I said softly.

He tipped my chin so that our eyes met. "I thought I'd been clear that I wasn't ever going to leave you again."

"J, a woman needs more than words. She needs to be shown that a man means what he says. You've been avoiding me, leaving early for work, coming home late and not having sex with me. I wasn't sure what to think because those are not the actions of a man who can't get enough of his woman."

He sighed. "You overthink this shit; you always have, babe. I don't say shit for the fucking sake of saying shit. You need to take it in that when I tell you something, I mean it."

"And you need to back up the shit you say with actions. Thinking is what women do. And yeah, sometimes we overthink stuff but that's only because the men in our lives give us mixed fucking signals."

"Mixed signals? Fuck, babe, women are the fucking masters of that shit."

"Well, let me just tell you that when your man who normally can't get enough of you stops wanting sex, that's the biggest mixed signal. So, I'm telling you, get that shit together otherwise we're going to have problems." I jabbed him in the chest as I said this.

A growl came from deep in his chest and he roughly pulled me to him. "Sweetheart, my cock will never get enough of you. Don't ever overthink that."

I reached up and pulled his face down to mine. "Show me," I whispered.

He didn't hesitate. His arms moved down my body and wrapped around my ass to lift me up. My legs wound around him as he backed me up against the wall. He bent his head and kissed me. Hard. Relentlessly. There was so much emotion behind this kiss and I took in the full force of his passion for me. It was his way of showing me that he meant what he'd said.

He ended the kiss and growled, "Nothing better than you, your legs around me, your pussy tight against me and your mouth on me, babe. I walk around with a fucking hard on for you every damn day, and as for other women, they're not even on my fucking radar anymore, sweetheart. Haven't been for over six years since I made you mine, and even when you weren't mine, none of them came close." His gaze intensified as he continued, "We clear on that now? Or do you need me to count the fucking ways I want to show you and your pussy how far gone I am?"

I sucked in a breath. If that wasn't clear, then I was a fucking moron. I murmured, "We're clear, baby."

He nodded. And then his gaze dropped to my chest. "Need to get these clothes off you, babe. Need your tits in my mouth. And then I'm going to eat you for fucking dinner."

I smiled. My man was back.

Chapter Four

Madison

I YAWNED AS I ENTERED THE KITCHEN THE NEXT morning and took in the sight before me. J was leaning against the kitchen counter, drinking coffee, and tracking my movements. To say this gave me tingles was an understatement. Last night after his declaration of love for me and my pussy, he'd taken me to bed and spent hours showing me how true his words were. This morning I was sore and exhausted, but in a good way. A very good way.

"You got the day off?" he asked after he scanned down my body and took in that I was dressed in shorts and a tank rather than work clothes.

"Yeah," I answered as I moved into his space.

He placed his coffee mug on the bench as I reached up and took hold of his face with both my hands. I stood on my tiptoes and kissed him. His mouth opened to let me in. His hands landed on my ass, and he drew me closer.

A moment later he groaned as he ended the kiss. "I've got to get to work, babe. Otherwise I'd lock you in our bedroom and continue this."

Smiling, I said, "Good to know."

His hands remained on me; he seemed reluctant to let me go and I liked that. This day was starting off good.

"What's your plans for the day?" he asked.

"I thought I might head over to the hardware store and look at paint. I want to paint the lounge room."

"What's wrong with the way it is now?"

My eyebrows shot up. "Really, J? The walls are off white. It's boring; we need some colour in the house."

I moved to the coffee machine and began making myself one while he finished his off. His eyes never left me. Just the way I liked it.

"I know what's going to happen. You're going to get all fucking excited about it, you might even start painting a bit of the wall, but I'm going to be the fucker that has to do most of it."

I gave him a pointed stare. "How do you know that?"

If J was the kind of man to roll his eyes, I was sure he would have done that right then. Instead, he muttered, "Gut instinct, babe. That, and twelve years of knowing you. Projects are your favourite thing, until they're not. And I'm betting this'll be the same."

He pushed off from the bench and rinsed his mug in the sink.

I chose to ignore what he'd said. He was kind of right, but there was no way I was admitting that. "So, I was thinking grey for the lounge room. With white."

He was back to watching me as I finished making my coffee and began making toast for breakfast. "Babe, knock yourself out. Just tell me when you need me to finish the job."

I scowled at him. "You can be an ass sometimes, you know that?"

He chuckled and closed the distance between us. "What can I say, you bring out the fucking best in me." He dipped his mouth to mine and gave me a quick kiss. "Gotta go, sweetheart."

He smacked me on the ass, and as he was heading out of the

kitchen, I called out, "You still haven't said anything about my hair."
It stung that he hadn't noticed it.

His head swung around to face me and he had a puzzled look
on his face. I noted his gaze moving to my hair and then to my face.
"Looks good."

"Oh my God, you didn't even notice that I've coloured it, did
you?"

"Madison, I've got no fucking clue about women and their hair.
It looks good, you look good." His gaze swept down my body and
he added, "When a woman's got legs like yours, a man's got no hope
of noticing their fucking hair, babe."

And that right there was J. He had a way of going from my bad
books to my good even when I was annoyed at him. All it took was
his dirty mouth to do it.

Jason

I'd taken half the day off work to spend the afternoon with
Madison, but standing here watching her flick through paint chips
made me wonder if I should have just let her come on her own. She
had six different ones and couldn't decide which one she liked best.
We'd been standing in this hardware aisle, going back and forth over
the colours for the past hour. I'd almost had enough but I was sure
that she could spend all fucking day doing this.

"Baby, do you think you can narrow it down some more? Like
to say, one?" I asked.

She scowled at me. "I knew you shouldn't have come with me.
You have absolutely no patience."

"I have a lot of patience, but you've been trying to decide
between these for an hour now."

"Well, I want to get it right, J," she muttered, throwing me a dirty look.

"Okay, how about this; if you pick one and hate it after we've painted, we can always paint it again."

Her eyes widened. "Really? You wouldn't mind?"

"No. So let's pick one and get out of here."

A pained look appeared on her face. "I really like two of them." She held up two and showed me. "Which one do you like?"

I grabbed them out of her hand and inspected them. "This one," I said, holding up the one I preferred. Fuck, why did women take so long to choose? I did it in three seconds flat.

She snatched them back out of my grasp, shaking her head. "You didn't even look at them, J."

"I did, babe. It's not fucking rocket science."

She gave me a pointed look. "You have no idea."

I blew out a breath. "I'm going to go outside and wait for you in the car. You reckon you can be done in five minutes?"

"I'll be as long as it takes. And you won't complain if you want more of what I gave you this morning."

Christ, she had me by the fucking balls. She'd given me the best goddamn head job this morning and I fucking needed more of that shit. "I'll be in the car, but hurry the fuck up because now all I can think of is your mouth and my cock." I leaned into her and promised, "I'll blow your fucking mind when we get home if you're done in five minutes."

As I pulled away from her, she curled her hand around my neck to bring me back to her, and murmured, "Baby, you always blow my mind, so there's no need for me to hurry."

I shook my head. "Fuck, we're gonna be here for another hour, aren't we?"

She held up a paint chip. "This one, J. And I'm not doing any of the work when you blow my mind. This one's all on you."

I grabbed the chip out of her hand and headed towards the

paint counter. My cock was so hard right now and I figured I could have her under me within fifteen minutes if the dude at the counter hurried his shit up.

★★★

Five hours later, Madison stood surveying the newly painted wall in our lounge room. The look on her face said it all. Finally, she turned to me with a grimace. "I don't like it."

I slowly nodded my head. "Yeah, I can tell."

"I'm sorry."

"All good, babe. You think the other colour would be better?"

"Yes, this one is too dark for the room. I thought it would be okay, but now I think the other colour won't be so dark. Do you mind if we repaint it? I know I'm being a pain."

I smirked at her. "Can I have that in writing? The bit about you being a pain."

She poked her tongue out at me, and I moved closer to her so I could pull her to me. Lowering my face to hers, I lightly kissed her lips and then said, "You would bore me to tears if you weren't you. I fucking dreamt of your pain in the ass ways while I was away."

I knew I'd said the right thing when she flashed a huge smile at me and replied, "That's biker talk for 'I love you', isn't it?"

I smacked her on the ass. "Yeah, sweetheart. Now, let's clean this shit up in here. I'll go to the hardware tomorrow and pick up the other paint. That okay with you?"

"That's great. Thank you."

She blasted me with another smile before she started cleaning up. Guilt sliced through me as I thought of the stuff I was keeping from her, about her father and what I'd done in Adelaide. This type of shit never bothered me before; I'd never had a problem separating club stuff and Madison, but for some reason, it was always on my mind now. As was the guilt that went with it.

"On second thoughts, I'll clean this up. You go and have a

shower. I'm taking you out tonight," I said, and she continued blasting me with that smile before finally leaving me to clean up and stew on my guilt.

★★★

"J, what movie do you want to see tonight?" Madison called out from the bedroom a couple of hours later.

I was in the lounge room watching the television and it irritated the fuck out of me when she yelled through the house, so I got up and walked into the bedroom before I answered her. She was lying across the bed with the laptop open, and greeted me with a smile.

"Babe, I fucking hate it when you do that," I said. I wasn't sure why I bothered though because I'd told her this enough times in the past for her to know it.

"Sorry, I'll try to remember that," she said with a sly look on her face.

Shaking my head, I muttered, "Yeah, I'm sure you will."

"So, which movie?"

"I don't even know what's on at the moment. Just pick an action flick cause we both like those."

"But there's that new one with Julia Roberts in it, the romantic comedy. It looks good."

My gaze travelled along her body, taking in the tight denim shorts she was wearing and her long legs they showed off. I'd rather be tortured with this sight all night, with no hope of getting those shorts off her, than watch a fucking romantic comedy. "Swear to God, Madison, you mention the words romantic comedy, and my fucking dick shrivels up."

She rolled off the bed and came to me, reaching one hand out to rub against my crotch. "J, your dick could never shrivel up. It was built to last forever. Why do you think I'm with you?"

Her touch was sending my dick crazy. It always fucking had. "Babe." I pinned her with a serious look. "You keep doing that and we're not making it to the movies tonight."

She stopped what she was doing but held my gaze. Her lips parted and her tongue ran over her lips. My eyes dropped to her lips and my breathing became uneven. After a moment, I looked back up to her face; it was flushed with desire and that sent a jolt of electricity through me. Straight to my already hard as fucking steel dick.

Her hands moved to my jeans and popped the button. And again, she stopped and watched me. I waited to see what she had in mind; this was becoming more enjoyable by the second, much more enjoyable than going to the movies, as far as I was concerned.

She reached down to her shorts, undid the button and then slowly slid the zip down. I watched as she pushed her shorts down, as they slid down her legs, and finally as she stepped out of them and kicked them to the side. I took my time moving my gaze back up to her face, letting it stop for a long while on her panties. When I finally found her eyes again, she was staring intently at me, waiting.

Her hand flicked out and she pointed a finger at my jeans, indicating for them to be removed. I shook my head, and pointed back at her, indicating for her to remove them. We waited, and watched. The air sizzled with sexual anticipation and my dick strained against my jeans. I desperately wanted to rip both our fucking clothes off and get inside her, but this game was turning me way the fuck on, so I resisted.

A sexy smile crept onto her face, and she gently ran her hand through her hair, pushing it off her face.

And we waited.

Eventually, she reached out and unzipped my jeans. Slowly. So fucking slowly, her eyes never leaving mine.

When she had them unzipped, she pushed them down and I stepped out of them. I had nothing on underneath them so my cock was free for her to do with it as she wished. And, Christ, I hoped she had plans for it.

But, she decided to tease me a little while longer, and stepped back from me. With her eyes still on mine, she lazily moved her hands to her t-shirt and very fucking slowly, removed it. My gaze went straight to her tits. I needed that bra off. Like yesterday.

She pointed at my shirt. I knew exactly what she wanted and decided to give it to her. My shirt hit the floor three seconds later. Our eyes locked. And we fucking waited.

I gave her about half a minute before I took charge. "Babe, that bra needs to come the fuck off. Now."

"If you want the bra or the panties off, J, you're going to have to make that happen."

Oh, I'd fucking make that happen. I moved to her and with both hands, I ripped her panties off in one movement. Her eyes widened with a mixture of shock and excitement.

I raised my eyebrows. "You want me to take the bra off too?"

"You rip it, you pay for a new one. And, baby, these weren't cheap," she replied, that sexy smile in place.

I ripped it. Then I grabbed her by the waist, and pulled her to me. "Best fucking money I've spent all day," I whispered in her ear.

We didn't make it to the movies that night. Instead, I showed her how much I loved her pussy. And how much I loved her.

Chapter Five

Madison

LATER THAT WEEK, I WENT TO SEE MY MOTHER. SHE WAS at home and seemed surprised by my visit.

"Been awhile since you've been here," she murmured as she let me in the house.

"Just came by to see that you're alright," I said. There was a distance between us, and I hated it. We'd always been close, until now. And I blamed my father for that.

"I'm fine. I wish you and your brother would start believing that." Annoyance crept into her voice and her body language spoke volumes; this was getting her down.

I followed her into the kitchen, taking in the messy state her house was in. This was unlike her and was another giveaway that she wasn't doing so good.

"Mum, how can you be okay? If I discovered that my husband had cheated on me throughout our marriage, and had another family, I'd be devastated and could never take him back. Add to that the fact he hits you..." I stopped because my emotions about this whole situation were getting to me; I was too damn mad about it and hurt for her.

She looked distressed at what I'd said but she quickly covered it. "I really don't want to talk about this with you," she snapped.

"Have you talked to anyone about it?"

"It's no-one's business, except mine and your fathers."

"Bullshit!" I yelled.

She flinched at my outburst, but didn't say a word.

"This affects our family, Mum. And damn it, I want to talk about it. I think there's been enough silence on the topic. I'm sick of the secrets and lies."

"I've tried to tell you that this lifestyle is full of fucking secrets and lies. It's time you started listening to me."

"Just because something's been a certain way forever doesn't mean it can't be changed. I don't expect everything to change, I get it, but this shit between you and Dad needs to be talked about. You need to talk; it must be eating you up inside. I know it would be eating away at me."

"You and I are different people, Madison. I chose this way of living when I married your father. I knew what I was getting myself into. What you've got with J appears to be different. I hope for your sake it is because otherwise he and the club will fucking eat you alive."

Fuck.

"So, you're telling me that you knew Dad was going to cheat on you? And did he hit you before you married him?" I was so confused; I just couldt imagine marrying a man like that.

She went quiet and took a minute before answering. "He did cheat on me before we married." She paused when she saw the look of disbelief cross my face. "You've got to understand that kind of thing was common; it still is in this life. You know that."

"I might know that but there's no way I'd ever marry a man who cheated on me, Mum."

She nodded. "I know that. And that does make me happy. I

just hope that J never goes there."

"Well, if he does, he won't have a dick left to do it again. Not after I get to him."

Mum laughed, and it was the best sound I'd heard all morning. It broke the tension a little. "I've missed you, honey," she said quietly.

My tone softened. "I've missed you too, Mum."

She pointed to the stool at the kitchen bench. "Have a seat and I'll make you a coffee."

Smiling, I said, "That would be good."

I sat, and she made coffee. We then spent the next couple of hours catching up and doing our best to avoid the topic of my father. I desperately wanted to talk to her about him some more, but I knew not to push her. If I did, she would retreat and start avoiding me. No, I needed to be smart about this and figure out a way to help her without her realising what I was doing.

★★★

I pulled up outside the clubhouse and sat in my car for a couple of minutes, processing some of the stuff my Mum had told me. She had willingly married a man who cheated on her. I was having trouble getting past that; it wasn't something I could do. My thoughts moved to J and our relationship. I trusted him. He'd proven himself and I truly believed he wouldn't cheat on me.

I was startled out of my thoughts when someone tapped on the window of my car. Looking up, I saw it was J. "Hey, baby," I greeted him, as I got out of the car.

He brushed his lips across mine and asked, "You okay?"

"Yeah. Kind of." I wasn't sure what I was feeling.

"What does kind of mean?"

I sighed. I wasn't sure why I'd come here after Mum's. Looking up at J though, I realised that I'd come for him. "It means that just being here with you is making me feel better already."

His eyebrows pinched together and he frowned. "Babe, I'm a

man. I need it spelt out for me sometimes. What the fuck's wrong?"

"J, you don't have the time to listen to all the shit swimming around in my head. I think I just needed to be near you."

"For the love of God, tell me what's wrong."

I searched his eyes; he had that concerned look he got when I was distressed. So, I decided to share. "I just spent some time with my Mum and she told me that she married my father knowing that he'd cheated on her. And she accepted it."

He didn't blink; didn't say or do anything. Just stood there, watching me and listening. When I didn't say anything else, he murmured, "It happens."

"It shouldn't!" I burst out.

"Madison, you know it happens."

"Yeah, well I'm stunned that my own mother put up with that shit."

"I'm not."

I didn't like the way this conversation was going. "Did you know about my father before it all came out?"

Again, he took his time, and when he finally answered me, he spoke slowly, deliberately. "I didn't know about Blade and his mother." He paused. "But I did know that Marcus liked to screw around."

My heart started beating faster. I didn't like what I was hearing. "What? You mean with other women besides Blade's mother?"

He nodded. "Yeah, with other women. He didn't hide it and I'm sure your mother knew. Babe, a lot of the guys fuck around; it's just up to the old ladies whether they turn a blind eye or move on."

"I know!" I puffed out a long breath. I knew all this shit, and normally I didn't even think about it, but this was my Mum we were talking about. "I fucking hate it, J, and if you do it, I'm not staying."

His nostrils flared and his tone hardened when he spoke. "Have I ever given you cause to think I'd cheat?"

Normally I'd pay attention to the tone he'd taken, but today I was focused solely on my mother and my feelings about her situation, so I missed the cues. "No, but I'm just saying, I won't stand for it."

Anger seeped into his voice. "And I'm just saying, don't fucking lump me in with your father. I haven't cheated on you and have no intention of ever doing it, so I don't fucking appreciate the attitude about it." He raked his fingers through his hair, shaking his head while he did it. And then he added, "I'm not your fucking father and I never will be."

I took a step back. J was furious and I wasn't sure where it had come from. He stood glaring at me. I madly tried to process what he'd said; it felt like there was something important here. "I know you're not, J. And I know you haven't cheated on me; I trust you."

He continued to glare at me, the vein in his neck pulsing. I had no idea what he was thinking so I waited, and didn't say a word. "Fuck," he muttered, and dropped his gaze to the ground. "This is fucking bullshit." It was like he was talking to himself so I still didn't say anything. He raised his face back to mine and I was stunned to see the anger had drained out of him, and instead he had an agonised look on his face. Something was tormenting him.

"What, baby?" I asked softly.

"I'm sorry," he said, and lightly grasped my cheek, rubbing his thumb back and forth over it.

I moved into him and put my hand on his chest. "What's going on, J? I know there's something bugging you, and I wish you'd talk to me."

His eyes searched mine; it was like he was weighing up whether to start talking or not. His chest heaved and he grabbed my hand off his chest, gave it a quick squeeze, and then said, "Nothing, babe. It's just club stuff."

Letting my hand go, he stepped back and said, "I have to get back to it. I'll see you at home tonight."

I was upset that he had again chosen not to confide in me, but I nodded and agreed, "Okay, I'll see you then."

He scrubbed a hand over his face, and nodded once before turning and walking back into the clubhouse with slumped shoulders and a downcast face.

I watched him go, with a heavy heart.

I felt helpless, and paralysed with fear as to what was going on with J, and what it was doing to our relationship.

★★★

"I truly feel like we're taking one step forward and three back at the moment," I admitted to Harlow the next morning over coffee. I'd just caught her up on me and J.

"How was he last night? Did he bring it up again?"

"No, he came home late, and he'd been drinking again. I'm so confused. J's not usually a big drinker but over the last couple of weeks he's been drinking more and more."

"Well, he's obviously keeping something from you. It really does sound like something is worrying him."

"He keeps saying it's just club business. Is Scott worried about club stuff at the moment?"

She shrugged. "He doesn't seem stressed about anything."

"Shit. It must be something else then, and he's just using that as an excuse."

"Sounds like it, honey."

"I feel like I'm in a catch twenty-two; I'm trying hard to not keep questioning him about shit but at the same time, if we don't talk about this, I feel like it's going to come between us."

"Yeah, I think you need to force the point. You guys are strong, right?"

My insecurities flared up. "He tells me that we are, and that we're forever, but sometimes his actions don't match up. And, to be honest, I would have thought we'd be engaged by now. When he got back two months ago, he was all about us getting married, and then nothing. So, I don't know what to think."

She gave me a sympathetic smile. "Sorry, hon. But I'm sure that if anyone can work this out, it's you and J. It's obvious to me that he loves you."

I smiled back at her. "Okay, that's enough about me. Tell me about you. How's my brother treating you?"

Her face lit up. "He's amazing."

I rolled my eyes. "The words Scott Cole and amazing have never been used before as far as I'm aware."

She laughed. "Well, I just did."

Nodding, I said, "You really do bring out the best in him."

"Did you know that he's booked Lisa's mum into rehab?"

"Really? When does she go?"

"It's at a place in Byron Bay and she leaves in a few days. Lisa's going to stay with him while she's away."

"Wow, that's great. How the hell did Scott get her to agree to that?"

"She came to him two days ago and begged for his help. He seems to think that she's serious about it so that's why he's agreed. It's costing him a fortune. See, I told you he's amazing."

I had to agree with her this time. "Yeah, who would have thought. But he does have that soft spot for Lisa."

"He does. She's such a gorgeous kid. I'm looking forward to girl time with her when she stays with him."

I laughed. "Don't you already have girl time with her? Scott was muttering something about paying for mani-pedi's for you two the other day. I didn't even know that he knew what a mani-pedi was."

"He didn't! But he does now," she said, winking.

"Oh my God, you're a classic, Harlow. Only you could get my brother to pay for mani-pedis."

She finished her coffee and smiled at me. "Amazing, I tell you. Don't tell him, but he's paying for high tea for me and Lisa this weekend."

"I can just hear him now, 'High fuckin' what, babe?'" I teased.

She started laughing so hard that tears came to her eyes, and this in turn, made me start too. "So true," she spluttered through her tears.

I checked the time on my phone. "I've got to go, but we're still on for tonight, right?"

"Definitely," she agreed, "I can't wait."

"Good. And thank you for this. I needed the chat and the laugh."

"Anytime. I love our chats."

I gave her a hug before I left, and thought about how thankful I was that she'd come into my life.

Chapter Six

Madison

I STOOD ON THE FOOTPATH AND WATCHED AS BLADE'S Jag came into view. He pulled up next to me, and I got in. I didn't look back at Harlow or Scott, although I could feel Scott's scowl behind me. My night out with Harlow had turned to shit, and I'd called on the one person I knew who was removed from the situation so I could get his take on it.

"Your house or mine?" he asked, eyes focused on mine in that intense Blade gaze I'd come to know well.

I sighed. "Mine."

He raised his brows.

"He won't be there, and I'm tired and want my bed," I said.

"Your call, babe," he replied, and then put the car in drive and focused his gaze on the road as he sped off.

We were both silent for the drive, and I appreciated him even more for that. It was one thing I'd learnt about him over the past few months; he was a perceptive man, and could read moods and needs very well.

I sat staring at the rain that had started falling. The darkness, the traffic lights and the rain all blurred together as I thought about the events of the night. I shivered from the air conditioning in the car, and Blade must have noticed because he reached out and shut it off. Normally, I would have thanked him for that, but tonight I just didn't have it in me.

Twenty minutes later we arrived at my house. No lights were on; J definitely wasn't home. I didn't move to unbuckle my belt, and Blade turned to me. "You sure you don't want me to take you to my place?"

I undid my belt. "No, I'm going to wait here until he comes home and then we're going to have it out."

He nodded and got out of the car. I waited because I knew that he liked to open my door. A moment later he came around to my side, and then we headed inside together. I switched on lights and made my way to the kitchen. Blade joined me a couple of minutes later; he'd inspected the house first which was something he always did.

I eyed him. "No boogiemen?"

He ignored me. "You gonna tell me what the fuck happened tonight?"

I indicated that we should sit, and when we were both settled, I said, "It's not just tonight."

He reached his arm up and rubbed the back of his neck as he studied me. Then he brought his arm down, rested it on the table, and leant forward. "Madison, you call me at midnight, distressed and crying. You don't tell me what's wrong, except to ramble on about J being an asshole. Then you beg me to come and pick you up. I get there and see that Scott was already on the scene but you've chosen to go home with me over him. That tells me that something fucked up has happened. And I want to know what it is, because I sure as fuck want to have a word with whoever upset you."

"It's J," I began, but started crying so didn't continue.

"What did he do?" he asked, his voice calm but firm.

I wiped my eyes and got my tears under control. Lifting my face to his, I said, "He was supposed to drop me off and pick me up, but he changed the plans at the last minute and got Scott to drop me off. He didn't even tell me; Scott just turned up. Then he didn't come to get me, and Scott said he'd take me home. When I rang J to see where he was, Griff answered the phone and told me that J had passed out drunk at the clubhouse."

Blade's body tensed and he balled his hand into a fist. "I thought you two were good; thought you were talking marriage."

I nodded. "So did I, but J's slowly pulled away from me since he got back. We seem to have hit crisis point this week, and now he's avoiding me."

"You've got no idea why?"

"No, he keeps telling me it's club problems but I don't think there are any real club problems. I think it's something to do with Dad."

Blade frowned momentarily. "You mentioned that you're going to have it out with him. Possibly not a good idea when he's drunk or hungover."

He was right, but I was so upset, angry and desperate for answers that I didn't think I could wait till he sobered up. "I know," I said softly, the tears threatening to fall again.

He watched me thoughtfully. "You're not being you," he stated.

"Huh?" I didn't understand what he meant.

"I haven't known you that long, but I've worked out that you're a hothead. You're very passionate, and your mouth goes off before your brain kicks into gear sometimes. And yet, you've let these problems with J go on for weeks without sorting it out. That doesn't seem like something you would do, babe. What gives?"

"I'm trying to change, trying to be better. I'm trying not to nag him about sharing stuff with me because it's caused us problems in the past."

He shook his head. "No."

"No, what?"

"No, you don't change who you are for someone. Those things I mentioned about you are you, Madison. The people who have chosen to love you have also chosen to accept those things. So, fuck it, you don't change for any-fucking-one."

I just sat there and stared at him. "But I really did cause problems in our relationship when I nagged him to tell me stuff."

"It takes two people to fuck up a relationship, not one. Sure, you don't need to nag him about shit, but babe, when the man you love is pulling back, there's a reason, and you have every fucking right to ask for that reason. And to keep asking until you get an honest answer."

I thought about what he'd said and I realised he was right. I'd wasted so much time and let J slowly slip through my fingers. This shit needed sorting out and I was going to do it; to hell with what J thought of me nagging him on this.

I wiped the leftover tears off my cheek, and smiled at Blade. "Okay, I'm going to sort this out with him tomorrow. Thank you."

He nodded. "Good."

Jason

I sat at the clubhouse bar and drank my coffee. Stalling. Time was ticking and I needed to go home and face Madison. I'd fucked up last night and now I had to try and put it right.

"So, you still haven't gone home?"

I turned to see Blade enter the room, a look of complete contempt on his face.

"None of your business, Blade," I muttered.

"It is my business, asshole, when it involves my sister. She phoned me crying her fucking eyes out last night. You need to get your shit together and sort out the mess you've created."

I turned to him. "And you need to stay out of shit that you know absolutely nothing about."

His eyes narrowed and he took the time to look me up and down. "You recovered fast from your hangover."

"Didn't have a fucking hangover."

"What's the real story then? Where were you last night when Madison thought you were here drunk? And I hope to Christ that answer doesn't involve another fucking woman."

"I'm going to let that one go. But just because you're Madison's brother doesn't give you the right to come in here and treat me like shit. If you must know, I was here last night, alone and sober," I snarled.

His forehead creased in a frown. "I'm listening."

I gestured at the chair next to me. "Take a seat, and let me tell you a fucking fairy tale about your father."

That got his attention and he sat, his full attention on what I was about to say. I proceeded to tell him about what happened in Adelaide. When I'd finished, he shook his head and murmured, "Jesus."

"Yeah," I agreed, "It's put me between a rock and a hard fucking place. I don't want to break Madison's heart even more where her father's concerned."

"Yeah well, I can tell you that if you don't share this with her, your days together are numbered. Marcus is a prick and she knows that. She can deal with this so long as she has you and the rest of us to support her."

I blew out a breath. He was right. "Okay."

"Today?" he pushed.

"Yeah, today." I stood up. "Give me your number in case she needs you later." I hadn't had a lot to do with Blade but I was starting to see what Madison saw in him; he genuinely cared for her.

We swapped numbers and then he left. I was just heading out myself when Marcus texted me. He wanted to see me in his office as soon as possible. He obviously had no clue I was here. I stalked into his office.

"What do you want?" I snapped at him.

He gestured to the seat in front of me but I remained standing. This wasn't a friendly meeting and I had no fucking intention of sitting with him for a chat.

Annoyance flashed across his face before he started talking. "Proved yourself while you were in Adelaide, J. Knew you had that darkness in you, just didn't know if you'd show it." I wasn't sure why he was sharing this with me now, two months after the fact.

I snarled at him. "The only thing I proved was what a cunt you are."

"No, you proved a whole lot more than that. And, I've got some more jobs for you coming up now that I know where your talents lie."

"You can take your fucking jobs and shove them up your fucking ass. I'm not your lap dog." My head was buzzing with the anger that he brought out in me; I was about ready to explode.

He stood up and leant both hands on the table, a threatening look taking over his face. "I'll remind you of those photos I have of you and the blonde in Adelaide. Perhaps that will encourage you to change your mind."

Fucker. "This conversation is over, asshole. And stay the fuck away from me and Madison. She doesn't want you in her life anymore and I sure as hell could do without being reminded of what a prick of a father in law I'm going to have one day."

"You don't seriously think that I'm going to allow her to marry you, do you?"

I studied him for a moment. He was fucking delusional if he thought he had any say in Madison's life anymore. "Try and fucking stop her."

"I won't have to; she'll come to that decision on her own after

I'm done with you."

"Like I said, stay the fuck away, Marcus. You think you pushed me in Adelaide? What I did there was for someone I didn't even fucking know. You don't want to know how far I'd go for someone I love." I had to get out of there; my rage towards him was only just being contained.

Leaving his office, I ran into Nash in the hallway. Christ, of all people. I scowled at him and continued walking.

"Hey, asshole," he called out.

I stopped and turned back to face him. "What?" I snapped.

"What the fuck's your problem?"

I stalked back to him. "You, motherfucker. I don't like the way you look at Madison. Never have. She's mine, so back the fuck off."

"You're a moody, jealous fuck, aren't you? Got no idea what you've got right in front of you."

"What the fuck does that mean?" Jesus, Nash could get under my skin without even trying but when he said shit like that, it really made my blood boil.

He leant his angry face closer to mine. "What it fucking means is that you've got a good woman doing her head in over you. You're right, she is yours; she's completely fucking yours but she doesn't feel it. So, instead of worrying about me, go home and worry about her."

Jesus, fucking Christ! Between Marcus and now Nash, I was itching to punch someone. My arm swung back, ready to take a shot. However, someone grabbed me from behind and stopped me.

"Not the way to settle this, brother," Scott warned.

I ripped my arm out of his hold. "Got nothing to do with you, Scott," I threw back at him, my furious glare still on Nash.

"I don't know what you two are arguing about but hitting a fellow club member brings problems into the club; problems we don't need."

"Fuck it!" I bellowed and stormed out of the clubhouse.

Madison

It was just after nine am when I heard J come through the front door. I'd been up waiting for him for two hours. In fact, I'd been considering going to the clubhouse and confronting him there.

His angry gaze swung my way when he entered the kitchen where I was waiting. I was stunned at his anger; he had no reason to be angry at me.

"We need to talk," I stated the obvious.

"Damn straight, we need to talk," he delivered on an angry breath.

I'd worked hard to contain my anger. All night, I'd bloody worked hard to do that; to wait to talk to him and find out his side of the story before getting angry. But now, I was done. "No! You don't get to be mad at me, J. I've not done anything wrong here," I yelled at him.

"You sure about that?" he asked, furious eyes blazing.

"Yes, I'm sure about that!"

"You spoke to Nash about us," he accused me.

Shit. I did feel guilty about that.

I raised my hands in a defensive gesture. "Hear me out, okay?"

He raked his fingers through his hair. "Start talking, Madison."

"Nash actually guessed there was something wrong and then when I hesitated to share with him, he guessed that you and I were having problems in the bedroom -"

He cut me off. "So, we don't have sex as much and that turns into us having problems in the bedroom?" he demanded. "Problems that you felt it necessary to talk to Nash of all fucking people about."

"If you'd calm down and discuss this rationally, you'd admit that, yes, we were having problems. You and I, we're people who need sex. Some people aren't like that but we fucking need it, J. It keeps us close. Nash pointed out that if we weren't having it, then it probably meant that our connection was somehow broken. So yeah, I'd call that problems in the bedroom."

I knew I'd said the absolutely wrong thing when his face twisted in barely concealed rage at the mention of Nash. He jabbed a finger in the air at me and warned, "Don't ever fucking talk to Nash about us again."

I struggled to keep check of my own anger. "Well I had to talk to someone because you sure as hell wouldn't talk to me!"

His eyes were wild, his face was flushed, and the vein in his neck was twitching. When J was angry, it consumed the room and I could feel it right down in my bones. He stood staring at me for awhile, not saying anything, until eventually he said, "I couldn't." And with those words, all the fight left him. He looked utterly broken, and unease filtered through me. Something was very wrong.

"Why?" I almost whispered, afraid of the answer. My legs felt shaky and chills surged through me. I reached out and gripped the top of the chair to steady myself. His eyes flicked to my hand on the chair, and then back up to my face. "Because I didn't want to shatter your world completely," he answered me softly. I didn't say anything, just stared at him, waiting for him to continue. He took a deep breath before going on. "Your father showed another side of himself to me while I was away, a side that you won't like, and I was trying to shelter you from that. Problem was that I was also trying not to have secrets between us. So, I've been fucking stuck between the two, not knowing how to proceed."

Relief coursed through me. I thought that he'd been going to tell me something about himself, something that would affect our relationship. This was better; this I could cope with. "You can tell me anything about my dad, J. I already know what an asshole he is."

"I know you think you hate him, but all that aside, he's your father. He's the fucking man who raised you. He should be the man you assess all other men by; the man who should always be setting an example for you. And as much as you don't want anything to do with him now, I'd have bet that over time you two would have found your way back. I fucking prayed for that, babe, because a life without a father in it fucking sucks. So, this shit I know now, it's probably gonna destroy any love you might have left." He paused and search-ed my face. "That's why I couldn't talk to you. That's why I was distant. I fucking wanted to be with you but I couldn't find the way to do that while I was keeping this secret."

My heart swelled with love for him. "I get it, baby," I said, and laid a hand on his chest. "But you can tell me now; I've got you to help me deal with it."

"Yeah, you do," he said, a sad smile threatening his lips. "Your father sent me to the Adelaide chapter, said he wanted me to check out a suspected paedophile in the club. Made out like he wasn't sure if the guy was that or not. Turned out that he'd known he was and he'd known that for about a year. Known what the cunt was doing and fucking let it happen. All so he could wait to use it against the guy when it suited his purpose. He also knew there were others. It makes me sick that he let that shit go on for a year."

My legs threatened to give way and I fought the rising bile. In that moment, I truly hated my father. I thought I already hated him as much as was possible but now I realised that J was right; I'd still had some love and hope there, but now, that was completely fading. "How could someone do that?" I gasped.

"I don't know, babe."

I had to sit; my legs couldn't support me anymore. J sat next to me, concerned eyes never leaving mine. "What did you do?" I asked him.

His chest rose and fell in a heavy movement. After a short moment, he said, "I killed him and two other guys. Not gonna detail that for you, sweetheart, but I don't want that a secret between us."

It didn't surprise me that he'd done that, and while thinking that, a horrible revelation came to me. "Dad played on your past didn't he? The stuff that happened to your cousin."

Pain flared on his face, and he nodded. "Yeah, he did."

"You said he waited till it suited his purpose. Why now?"

"The guy was the VP and was blocking a drug deal that the President wanted passed. Marcus helped him achieve that by using me."

My mind was racing to process all this. "Where are you and Dad at now?"

"He told me today that he wants me to do some more jobs for him. I'm not though. I'm done with him. And if he wants me out of the club, he can fucking fight for that because I'm not backing down and I'm not leaving."

"Scott won't let that happen."

"No, but your father has an agenda, babe. He told me he won't let me marry you."

Butterflies hit my stomach at his words. "We're getting married?"

His forehead creased. "Of course, we're fucking getting married. Told him he's got no say in it."

I smiled; a huge smile, because in amongst all the awful stuff he'd told me, he'd given me the one thing I really needed to hear. I leant my face to his and lightly kissed him. "He's got no say in it," I promised.

Now he smiled. "I know." His hand curled around my neck and he rested his forehead against mine. "Fuck babe, it feels so good not to have all that shit between us anymore; as much as I hate you having to deal with it."

My arms circled him. "I'm glad you finally told me. I was beginning to go insane wondering what the hell was going on with you."

We sat there like that for a long time. I savoured the closeness and the feeling of fresh beginnings. J was finally mine again; completely mine. I chose to focus on this for the moment rather than on the sense of loss I felt over my father.

Chapter Seven

Jason

I SAT BACK AND WATCHED MADISON, BROOKE AND Crystal, and not for the first time this week, I realised I was a lucky bastard. It had been almost a week since I'd finally told Madison about her father, and while it'd been a long fucking week dealing with the emotional fallout of that, it'd also been a fucking fantastic week with her.

"J, earth to J," Brooke called, interrupting my thoughts.

"What?"

She shook her head. "You keep zoning out on us. You okay?"

"He's probably thinking about club business; it's always just club business," Madison teased with a wink. "Brooke wants to know if we want to go to the movies with her and Crystal next Thursday night instead of doing Thursday night dinner."

Thursday night dinners had become our new tradition. Brooke and Madison had started it while I was away and they made sure I was there every week; my life wasn't fucking worth living if I didn't make it. "Sure," I agreed, "Whatever you want."

Brooke rolled her eyes. "J, you can say no if you'd rather just stick to dinner. It's a kids movie after all."

Fuck me. I hated kids movies. "All good. I'll be there." I looked at Crystal to see her staring intently at me. "What are we seeing, kiddo?"

She hit me with a mega smile. "It's a dog movie. You're going to love it, J."

Christ, a fucking dog movie. I plastered a smile on my face for her. "Looking forward to it, sweetheart." Crystal was a good kid; she was still trying to get over her mother and brother's deaths, and the three of us were working hard to help her. Building a strong family was part of that so a dog movie was the least I could do.

We finished dinner and Brooke insisted I help her clean up while Madison helped Crystal with an assignment for school.

"You and Madison seem a hell of a lot happier this week," she said as we did the dishes.

"Yeah," I agreed. I hadn't mentioned anything about our problems to Brooke so I wondered where this was coming from. "Did Madison say something to you?"

"No, I've got no idea what's been going on with you two but there's definitely been tension for the last couple of weeks. You two alright?"

"We are now. Been a long few months but we're working on it." I hated talking about this shit but Brooke was like Madison and invested copious amounts of fucking energy into trying to get me to talk.

She didn't fail me today. "When are you going to ask her to marry you? I thought you'd have that all done by now, the bossy ass that you are."

"We had shit to sort out," I muttered.

"And have you sorted it now?"

"Fuck, Brooke. Yes, it's fucking sorted."

She turned and looked at me intently. "Good, because I want to see you happy, big brother. You two have been through so much crap and I, for one, want you to get your happy ending. You and I were dealt a crappy hand with our family; Madison changed our luck."

"Shit." She'd stunned me. "I didn't realise you were such a huge fan of Madison's after all the shit from years ago."

"I spent a lot of time with her while you were away and we wiped the slate clean. You've seen us together; I thought you knew we were closer now."

"I've been preoccupied. I also thought you were just making an effort for Crystal and me."

"Nope. She's good for you and she's given both of us the family we never had. Plus she seems to have gotten herself together and worked out how to handle you. I'm surprised she put up with whatever you two had going on between you for so long."

"Yeah, you and me both."

"So, when are you proposing?"

"Soon."

She smiled at me. "Good. And then we can have some little J's running around."

I grinned at her. "Fuck, we'd drive Madison fucking insane if we had more of me running around. How soon do you reckon I can make that happen?"

★★★

"Babe, how much longer are you gonna be in there?" I called out to Madison. She'd been in the bathroom for a long fucking time doing her face or some shit, and I'd been waiting for her to come to bed. My patience was running out.

"Not long. Why?"

"You never finished what you started this morning, and I'm more than fucking ready for you to do that." My cock had been hard for her all day, and she'd been at work. Then we'd had the dinner at Brooke's tonight so there'd been no time when she got home from work. The fucking universe had been against me today.

She appeared in the doorway between the bathroom and the bedroom, hand on hip. "May I just remind you that I never finished what I started because *you* got called into work early?"

Fuck, she was so sexy when I managed to rile her up. I grinned. "You could have finished me off real quick but you didn't want to."

Her mouth fell open. "You're an ass, J. Sure I could have finished you off but what about me?" She shook her head and turned around to walk back into the bathroom, muttering something about bastards and hand jobs. I fucking loved her sexy mouth and hotheadedness.

I left her alone for a couple of minutes before heading into the bathroom to see what she was doing. The sight that greeted me almost made me come on the spot. She'd stripped and was standing naked in front of the sink. Currently, she was raised up on her toes and leaning forward to look in the mirror which meant her ass was up and out. I zeroed in on that ass and started walking towards her so I could get my hands on it.

"Stop," she ordered.

Shit. Madison doing bossy was a turn on. I did what she said and found her gaze looking back at me in the mirror.

"Touch my ass and you'll be going without tonight," she said.

I raised my eyebrows and folded my arms across my chest. Smirking at her, I said, "Sweetheart, I'm not going without tonight."

She raised her brows back at me. "Oh really, J? Got that hand ready, have you?"

"Don't need it; got something better. Something that never fucking says no to me."

"And that would be?"

I moved to her, my front brushing up against her back, and slid my hands around her waist, letting them dip down to her pussy. Running a finger between her wet lips, I murmured in her ear,

"This."

Her head fell back on my shoulder and she moaned. Then she murmured back to me, "I think I love you."

I moved my face to brush my lips across her temple, and thrust my finger in further and with more force. "You think?"

"Well, we could move it up to a 'I know for sure' with a little more coaxing."

I withdrew my finger, and lightly circled her clit before stopping altogether. "How about without a little coaxing? You think it would take long for you to admit it?"

She didn't miss a beat. "I'd probably admit it a whole lot quicker if you were to take that cock of yours that I love and show me what you can do with it."

Fuck. My cock was straining against my pants, more than ready to show her, but I wanted to take her to the edge and make her cave first. I moved my hand to her nipple and rubbed it. "My cock wants to hear your words just as much as I do, baby."

She swivelled around to face me. Her hand went to my dick but I caught it and stopped her. I realised that Madison's game playing skills were much better than mine when she began touching herself with her other hand. My gaze moved to her pussy instantly; I was a fool for her when she touched herself.

"Fuck, you play dirty, woman," I growled, and dropped to my knees and pushed her hand out of the way. My tongue darted out to lick her pink lips and my hands grasped her ass, pulling her sweet pussy to my mouth.

Her hand grabbed my hair, she moaned, and then murmured, "I know I love you, J."

I groaned. This had started out as me telling her that I wanted her to finish what she'd started this morning. Now here I was, on my knees and at her mercy. My woman fucking owned me.

Chapter Eight

Jason

"J, I'M BUSY. I DON'T HAVE TIME TO GO FOR A RIDE WITH you today. Dinner at Brooke's last night meant that I didn't get any housework done that I really needed done by tomorrow." Madison argued with me in the frustrated tone she reserved for when she was especially annoyed at me rather than just mildly annoyed at me.

I wasn't taking no for an answer though. "Too bad. You're coming," I said forcefully, in the tone that I used when I wasn't giving her a choice.

Her head snapped up from the dishes she was doing. "So you're going to help me finish off the housework when we get back? I want this house spotless when everyone comes over tomorrow."

At this point, I'd have promised her the fucking world just to get her on the back of my bike this afternoon. "Yes."

She lifted her hand out of the water and pointed her finger at me, splashing water on the floor. "Okay, but you promised, so I'm not letting you out of it."

I nodded in a hurry the fuck up motion. "Let's move this along, babe. Running out of afternoon the longer we stand here."

She blew out an exasperated sigh, and muttered, "Not sure why this is so important that we have to do it right now."

I smacked her on the ass, my anxiety to get her moving reaching an extreme level. "Now, babe. We gotta go."

★★★

An hour later we arrived at our destination, and Madison turned to me in surprise after she got off the bike and removed her helmet. "We haven't been here for ages," she said softly.

I ran my thumb over her cheek. "Yeah, thought it was time."

Her face slowly broke out in a smile. I got off the bike and grabbed her hand, and led her to the clearing. The view from Mt Glorious always stunned me. I could sit here for hours just staring at the view and thinking about shit. I moved behind her, put my arms around her and leant my chin on her shoulder. We didn't say a word; didn't need to. This was our place and all we needed was each other and the silence.

Eventually, I murmured, "I love you, Madison Cole."

I couldn't see it, but I could hear the smile in her voice when she said, "I love you too, Jason Reilly."

I moved my arms so that I could turn her around to face me. My eyes searched hers and I dipped my head and kissed her. Slowly. Deeply.

We pulled apart, and I said gruffly, "This is where I decided to make you mine."

She nodded. "I know, baby." Her hand rested on my chest, and I moved my hand around to rest on her ass. She smiled at that; she couldn't get enough of that, and neither could I. I knew I never would.

"This is where I'm gonna make sure you're mine forever."

Her eyes widened and her face flushed with colour.

I kept one hand on her ass and with the other, I reached into my pocket and pulled out the little blue box I'd been carrying around for fucking weeks. Reluctantly, I had to move my hand off her ass because I needed it to open the box. I flipped the lid to reveal a diamond ring that cost me a small fucking fortune.

Her breathing had picked up and her chest was rising and falling fast. And there was a huge fucking smile on her face.

"Baby, will you make me the happiest fucker on this planet by marrying me?"

She grabbed the ring off me and shoved it straight on her finger, then jumped up into my arms and wrapped herself around me. After she kissed me hard, she breathed out, "Yes."

I held onto her for a little while longer and then let her down. "Thank fuck," I said.

She frowned slightly. "You knew I'd say yes, right?"

"Sometimes you make me work for it, babe, so I wasn't sure if today would be one of those occasions."

She held up her hand with the ring on it. "J, I'd say you nailed it with this baby," she said, grinning, but then her face took on a serious look, "There's no way I was ever saying no to you. I wasn't letting you go again. We're a forever deal now, okay?"

"Trust me, sweetheart, you haven't got a hope in hell of ever getting rid of me."

"Ditto," she said.

She reached out and hugged me, and I let my hands run up and down her body. And I decided I really was the happiest fucker on Earth right now.

Chapter Nine

Madison

"SHOW ME THAT RING!" HARLOW EXCLAIMED, GRABBING my hand. "Oh my God, it's huge! And how did he know that you love Tiffany rings?"

Before I could answer, Brooke wandered into the kitchen where we were, and interjected, "I might have had something to do with that. Not that I realised it at the time, but I was browsing the Tiffany website one day when J was at my house. I casually mentioned something about you loving a particular ring. Remember, you showed it to me once?"

I nodded. "Yes, I do remember. Thank God for that! And shit, he actually paid attention to what you said." I was so impressed with J at the moment, and he was reaping the rewards of that; we'd had so much sex last night and this morning that I wasn't sure I had the energy to get through this party.

"Where's the birthday boy?" Brooke asked.

I pointed towards the backyard. "He's out there." I squinted to try and see where he was but I couldn't find him. "I think he's out there."

"Cool, I'll go in search of," she said, and left us to it.

"So, I saw Nash here," Harlow said, surprise in her voice, "I wasn't sure that J would invite him."

"Yeah, me either. That's still a touchy subject but I've told J once and for all that he needs to get that shit under control. He seems to be working on it."

"Scott said, and I quote his words, 'It's a lot fucking easier to work with those assholes when they're not being dicks'".

I laughed. "Yeah, I bet he did."

The back door slid open and Nash graced us with his presence. He grinned at us. "My two favourite girls."

"What will you call us once you find a woman, Nash?' I teased him.

"Never gonna happen, sweet thing, so we're all good."

"I hope it does happen for you, Nash. She'd be a lucky woman," Harlow said.

He beamed at her. "Means a lot, babe. Now, have either of you seen Griff? It's his fuckin' birthday and none of us can find the fucker."

"No, I thought he was out the back with you guys," I said.

"He was but none of us have seen him in the last twenty minutes or so," Nash muttered. "If you see him, tell him I'm looking for him."

He headed down the hallway towards the front door. As he left, Lisa and Crystal ran past him, past us and out the back door. I heard him laugh and say, "Christ, it's a fuckin' madhouse here today."

I reached into the cupboard and passed Harlow the potatoes for the potato salad we were making. She began peeling them while I grabbed the ingredients for a caesar salad out of the fridge and started on that.

The front door slammed and a minute later, Scott entered the kitchen. Harlow smiled up at him and he reached for her, giving her a quick kiss on the lips. "You taste so good," he murmured quietly.

Then he let her go and gave his attention to me. "Gonna prepare you now, Dad's on his way."

My heart froze. I shook my head. "No, you've got to stop him. Tell J, he'll stop him." I was panicked. I hadn't spoken to Dad for awhile now and had been ignoring his calls for the last few days.

"I would tell J, but I can't find him. Can't fuckin' find Griff either."

I frowned. "They were here before."

"Yeah, but nowhere to be found now. Look, when Dad gets here, I'll do my best to get rid of him but you know what he's like. I can't guarantee anything."

"Is Mum with him?"

"Don't think so."

"J told me what he did," I said.

He nodded. "I know."

"Does Mum know?"

"I haven't told her and I doubt that J has. So, if you haven't either, then no."

I made a decision that I'd been toying with ever since J shared the information with me. "I'm going to tell her."

"Your call. I don't think it'll motivate her to leave him but you never fucking know."

I was about to say something else but we were interrupted by the rumble of a bike.

Scott gave us a pointed look that said 'stay here', and then stalked down the hallway to the front door.

I turned to Harlow. "Where the fuck is J?" I needed him like I hadn't needed him for a long time.

She passed me my phone. "Ring him," she urged.

He answered on the third ring. "Babe, I'm out the front with your father. Stay inside while we get rid of him, okay?"

Relief hit me. "Thanks, baby," I said softly and hung up.

My gaze swung to Harlow who was watching me through

concerned eyes. "J's outside."

She smiled tightly, and then looked out the back. "I'm going to round up these kids and get them inside."

"Good idea." I watched her go, not sure why I had such an intense feeling of unease in the pit of my stomach. When I heard lots of yelling out the front, it only intensified. I was rooted to the spot, but when the yelling continued, I was drawn to the front door.

I opened the front door and found my father outside with J, Scott, Nash and Griff. Scott was holding J back and Nash had my father. The fury on all their faces was clear. But the man who was radiating the most anger was Griff. This really didn't surprise me; he scared me at the best of times.

"Marcus, this is fucking bullshit and you know it," Griff snarled at my father.

Dad's attention turned to me, and then back to Griff. "It's not fucking bullshit, and besides, why don't we let Madison be the judge of that. She's the one who seems to think J is the man for her. The least we can do is give her all the information."

I looked at J who had a feral look in his eyes and was struggling against Scott. If Scott let him go, I knew he'd knock my father out or worse. I needed to end this now, for J's sake more than anyone's.

I stepped outside and walked to where Nash had Dad. It took everything I had but I looked him in the eyes when I spoke. "Spit it out and then get the hell out of here. I don't want you here."

He tried to get out of Nash's hold, but Nash pulled him back tighter, and barked, "Say whatever you came to say and then you can do what Madison says and leave."

Dad eyed me, and jerked his head towards J. "He tell you what he got up to while he was away?"

"If that's what you came to tell me, you could have saved yourself a trip because, yes he did tell me. And I think even less of you for that than I did before he told me. In fact, you don't even exist for me anymore."

He flinched, and then his face contorted with rage. "So you know about the blonde piece he had on the side while he was away? And you're still going to marry him?"

My eyes flew to J and my heart began beating wildly. J's gaze was on me; steady. He still had that feral look in them but they were steady; sure. And he shook his head once. And in that instant, I knew.

I turned back to my father. "Nothing you say can or will come between me and J. I know he loves me; only me. In fact, I've never been so sure of that in my life, so take your lies and your pathetic attempts at breaking us up, and leave us the fuck alone."

Dad went to say something else, but Nash shoved him away, and said, "You've said what you came to say, now it's time to leave."

I walked over to J, and he pulled me close, his arm around my shoulder. "You okay?" he asked quietly.

"Yeah, baby," I answered, smiling up at him.

He bent down and kissed me. "I love you," he said when he ended it.

I laid a palm on his cheek. "I love you, too."

Chapter Ten

2 months later
February

Jason

"DID YOUR MUM CALL YOU YET, BABE? LET YOU KNOW what she's doing tomorrow?" I asked Madison as she packed her overnight bag.

"Yeah," she said quietly, "She's coming to both the wedding and reception. Said that Dad's going away for a couple of days so he won't bother us. She raved on with some bullshit about how he loves me enough to give me that. I still can't believe that even after I told her what happened in Adelaide, she chooses to stay with him."

I breathed a sigh of relief. Thank fuck he wouldn't be there. I knew that Madison was torn about it though. I moved from the doorway to where she was at the bed, and placed my hand on her back. "You okay?"

She stopped what she was doing and turned to me. Her face was a mess of emotions. I knew tears weren't far off. "I don't know why I feel this way, J. I don't want him there; don't want him in my life. And yet, it's like there's this hole in my heart and I miss him. I want him there. It doesn't make any sense."

I nodded and drew her close, wrapping my arms around her. Lowering my head, I kissed her on the forehead. "Baby, he's your father. You'd have to have a heart of ice to not have these feelings. You want the version of him that you grew up with there; the father you loved before you discovered who he really was."

Her tears came and her body shook with sobs. I held her, and didn't say anything else. I'd been waiting for this to happen for months but Madison had locked it away and done her best to move on without him in her life.

After awhile, she looked up at me through teary eyes. "You're right, I do want him there, just not the him that he is to me now. Most days, I just want to go back in time and not know all this shit."

"Trust me babe, I'd fucking like that too."

"I never stopped to really think what it must have been like for you growing up with your parents. And we've hardly spoken about it."

Heaviness settled in my chest. "Baby, it's the day before our wedding. Do we really want to bring this shit up today?"

She nodded. "Yeah, J, we do. It's been on my mind for awhile now, and I want you to talk to me about it."

I blew out a long breath. Talking was something we were getting better at. I fucking hated it most of the time, but even I had to admit it helped us. And it really seemed to help Madison. Between us talking, her attendance at AA, and time spent building family with Brooke, Scott and Harlow, she was doing so much better these days. I remained vigilant, and kept my eye out for any signs that she was backsliding. However as the days passed, I could see her growing stronger.

"It fucking sucked, growing up with an alcoholic mother. And for her not to take any of my help was a kick in the guts. My last year in school was spent making sure she was still alive every fucking morning, and being the parent to Brooke that neither of mine were. My father was off gambling and screwing his way through Brisbane. He only came home every few days. He'd bring us food, push Mum around a bit and fight with her, and then take off again."

"What went wrong between them?"

"They were happy until about the time I was twelve. Mum fell pregnant with her third child and they were both over the fucking moon about that. Then she lost the baby. They never came back from that because Mum ended up with depression and shut Dad out. Slowly over the years, they drifted apart. Mum began drinking and Dad started staying out gambling. It was fucking awful, babe. How two people can go from being completely in love to what they became is beyond me. Dad started looking at Mum like she was the shit he scraped off his shoes. And Mum didn't even look at him most of the time; it was like he didn't exist for her anymore."

"No wonder you hated my drinking," she said, her voice cracking.

"It's a disease that takes so much from a person. It took my mother's spirit and then it took her family, and at the end it took her fucking life. I don't want that for you. And I don't fucking want that for us. I struggled with my love for her and my hatred of what she was doing to herself and to us. The day she crashed that car and killed herself and my father was one of the worst days of my life. And yet, I felt a sense of fucking relief. I hated that about myself. But after years of watching it destroy our family, and shatter Brooke's life, it felt like a fucking weight had lifted."

"You never know what's going on in someone's life, do you?" she mused.

"No," I agreed.

"I mean, I knew you back then but at the same time, I didn't. You joined Storm just after your parents died and there you were, coping with their death and looking after Brooke. I had no idea."

She paused and searched my eyes. "Why have we never taken the time to talk about this?"

"Baby, you and I spent too many years screwing and arguing to get into this shit. You knew the basics and, trust me, that was enough for me. I don't talk to anyone about this stuff. Even Brooke and I hardly discuss it. What's the fucking point? It's in the past; I only want to look forward."

"Yeah, well I was a shit girlfriend to you, and for that, I'm sorry."

"I think as people get older, and have crap happen to them, they open their eyes more; see shit for what it really is. That's where you're at with all this stuff going on between you and your family. And believe me, sweetheart, you weren't a shit girlfriend; you were exactly what I needed and still are."

She sighed. "I'm so glad we didn't give up on each other. What we have now is good; so good, baby."

I couldn't fucking agree more. "Yeah, it is," I said, and then to lighten the mood, I gave her what I knew she loved from me, "Now, you've gotta finish packing that bag so that I can take you to Harlow's. And make sure you don't bother with any underwear tomorrow because after a night away from you, I don't need any-fucking-thing coming between me and your pussy."

Her eyes lit up. "I love your dirty mouth, J." And then she stood on her toes and breathed into my ear, "I don't have any underwear on right now, baby."

Fuck me, I loved this woman.

★★★

"You got a moment?" Blade asked as I opened my front door to him.

"Sure," I said, gesturing for him to come in.

"Madison home?"

"No."

We made our way to the kitchen and then he turned to look at me.

"I don't really know you, J, but you're marrying my sister so I'll be taking the time to rectify that."

I nodded; I agreed with that fully.

He continued, "While you were away, Madison shared a lot with me. That woman loves you with her heart and soul. Only a lucky man gets that in his lifetime and you, my friend, are that lucky." He paused and assessed me with his hard gaze.

"You gonna get to the point, Blade?" I was getting impatient with where he was going with this.

"Don't fuck it up. Don't take what she's giving you and trample it, because if you do, I'll be the one you'll deal with."

I nodded. "Yeah, I understand that about you, brother. And I'm with you all the way. Madison's lucky to have you looking out for her. But you need to know that I have no intention of fucking this up. She and I have worked too damn hard to get this far; not gonna screw that up."

He processed that silently for a moment before saying, "Good."

I decided I liked him as he was leaving; anyone who cared for Madison like he did was someone I had time for.

★★★

"Tomorrow's been a long time coming," Scott muttered as he leant back in his chair and stretched his arms up, hands behind his head.

I took a swig of my beer. "Yeah it has, brother," I agreed.

It was nearly midnight, nearly my wedding day, and Scott had dropped in earlier for a beer. Madison was at Harlow's place with Serena, and Brooke, and my dick was fucking missing her. Christ, at this rate, I'd be throwing her over my shoulders after she promised me forever, and saying to fuck with the reception.

"Madison texted me to say Dad wouldn't be there. She coping alright?"

"It's fucked, Scott. I could kill him for what he's done to her."

He nodded, deep in thought. Then he leant forward and rested his arms on his legs. "Lotta shit going down with the club right now. When you get back from your honeymoon, it'll be time to fix that."

"What's your plan? You want Marcus out?"

"Yeah, I fucking want him out. We need to figure out what he's up to and at the moment, I'm no closer to that answer. He's good at covering his tracks."

"I'm betting it's got something to do with the Adelaide chapter. Look there."

"I've got Nash on that. And Griff's finally come around to my way of thinking. He's been loyal to Dad for so long but he's lost all respect now. Between him and Nash, I reckon they'll come up with something soon."

"Good. I'll be back in two weeks and the sooner we can take that fucker down, the better."

"We're watching your back too, brother. Have a feeling that Dad wants you out."

"Appreciate that. I've come to the same conclusion".

He finished his beer and then stood to leave. "I'll be over at about ten tomorrow morning. I'm making sure you get to that wedding."

"Wedding's not till two, brother," I reminded him.

"I'm not taking any fucking chances. The last thing I need is Madison pissed because either a, you're late, or b, you don't fucking show at all."

"No need to worry. There's no way that woman isn't ending tomorrow as my wife."

He grinned. "True. You two are gonna live to an old age pissing the shit outta each other."

Now it was my turn to grin. "Too fucking right."

Chapter Eleven

Madison

"Oh my God, you look beautiful!" Serena exclaimed.

I turned to look at my reflection in the mirror. The dress I'd chosen for today was white with a corset top and a puffy tulle skirt that fell to the floor. The tie for the top was at the side and I'd incorporated a strip of black fabric there. I'd used black leather string to tie it and made this long so that it hung down over the tulle skirt. There were black jewels scattered throughout the top and these were gorgeous when the light caught them.

I turned back to the girls who were all watching me, and asked, "You think J will like it?"

"Fuck yes!" Serena exclaimed, and we all laughed. "With your boobs popping out of that top like that, he won't be able to control himself."

"You look beautiful too," I said to Serena who was my only bridesmaid for the day. J had chosen to have Scott as his best man, with no other groomsmen, so I'd agreed to just one bridesmaid.

She looked down at her black dress; it was an above the knee halter dress with a plunging neckline that showed off her ample cleavage. She'd paired it with stunning black strappy heels. Looking back up at me she asked, "So, you think I might get lucky with one of these biker dudes? Cause I gotta tell you, I need to break the drought."

"Honey, you'll have Nash eating out of your hands the minute he lays eyes on you," Harlow promised.

Serena looked enquiringly at me. "I don't think I met Nash at Christmas when I visited, did I?"

"No, he spent Christmas with his family. Harlow's right, Nash will be beside himself when he sees you."

Serena's eyes sparkled. "Sounds good, chica. For the love of God, tell me he's hot. And tattooed. I fucking want tattoos on the next man I bang."

Brooke laughed out loud. "You and Nash are so suited it's not funny. That totally sounded like something he would say."

Blake cut in, "Ladies, let's get back to getting ready for this wedding. I don't really want to hear about banging a hot biker dude." He turned to me and asked, "Is there anything else you need me to do for you, baby doll?"

I smiled up at him. "No, you've done so much already." He really had. He'd organised the catering for us, and had brought some of his restaurant staff up to Brisbane for the reception. We were having an outdoor wedding at Mt Glorious after the place on the river I'd wanted fell through at the last minute. They'd double booked and screwed us around so J had found an alternative venue for us.

"There's nothing I wouldn't do for you, babe." His eyes softened, and he added, "I actually think that J's going to make you very happy. Can't fucking believe I'm saying that, but I'm man enough to admit when I'm wrong."

I grinned. "Thank you! I'm just glad you two get along now. Makes my life much bloody easier."

The rumble of a bike outside distracted us from our conversation. I had no idea how we were getting to the wedding because J had taken care of those plans for me, but I figured it would probably be on the back of a bike. We all headed outside to find two bikes waiting at the curb. I was surprised to see Nash walking up the path to us. Griff was with him, and that didn't surprise me, but I'd never in a million years thought J would send Nash. They were wearing jeans, t-shirts and their cuts.

Serena's eyes hit mine; she looked panicked. "Don't tell me I have to get on the back of a bloody bike in this dress?"

Nash pulled his shades off and grinned at her. His eyes swept down her body and then slowly made their way back up to her face. "Unfortunately not, sweet thing, but I'd be more than happy to put you on the back of my bike after the wedding."

I looked at Serena to see her giving him the once over too. She hit him with a flirty smile. "You must be Nash."

"My name on your lips is the best fuckin' thing I've heard all week."

"These girls weren't lying," she murmured, not taking her eyes off him.

He cocked his head to the side. "How's that, sweet thing?"

"I told them I needed a hot, tattooed biker boy for tonight, and they said you'd probably be up for it."

Nash sucked in a breath and swung his eyes to me. "Fuck, Madison, where you been hiding this chick?"

I rolled my eyes. "Nash meet Serena, Serena meet your new biker boy," I hurriedly introduced them, "Now, what's the plan here, Nash? There are only two bikes but four of us."

He raised his hands in a defensive gesture. "Settle, babe. We've got it under control."

At that moment, a black Jag eased its way in to park behind the bikes, and Blade stepped out. He directed his gaze to me but I couldn't see his eyes as they were hidden behind a pair of dark aviators. As he walked towards me I noted that he was dressed in black jeans, t-shirt and suit jacket, and heavy black boots.

He joined us and took his sunglasses off. His eyes were soft as they took me in. "You look beautiful, babe," he murmured.

I loved it when he was soft and as this wasn't often, I savoured it. Smiling up at him, I said, "Thank you."

He turned his attention to Nash. "You've got Madison, and the girls are with me, yeah?"

Nash nodded. "Yeah."

Griff stepped in, his intense eyes focused on me. "Time's running out. You ready to go, Madison?"

"Yes," I said, expecting nerves to hit my stomach. I'd been expecting them today because it's what I'd been told to expect on my wedding day. But I didn't feel nervous at all. For the first time in a very long time, I felt calm and sure.

Marrying J was exactly what I was supposed to be doing today.

★★★

"You ready, sweetheart?" Blade asked me, looping our arms together and holding my hand.

I smiled at him. "More than you know."

I lost him for a moment. His gaze became unfocused; something very unlike Blade. Then he came back to me and softly said, "I've come to see that you and J were made for each other, and I understand that type of love; the kind that only fate brings."

I nodded at him; I was too emotional to say anything because I knew that Blade was referring to his fiancé who had died.

He squeezed my hand. "Let's get you married."

My heart expanded as I took in the scene before me. Blade and I were about to walk up the 'aisle'; a grassy walkway created by bikes parked on either side. At the end was a marquee and our guests were standing in front of that. J was up there; I could see him, and my belly did somersaults as I watched him watch me.

Blade took a step and I followed, and a song began playing.

3

There were speakers set up and I could hear it clearly, and my heart almost burst out of my chest. J hadn't wanted much to do with planning our wedding but he'd asked to be in charge of a couple of things. One was my transportation to the wedding and the other was the music. He'd been especially adamant that he wanted to choose the song for me to walk down the aisle to and the song we had our first dance to.

The song he'd chosen was "I Will" by Matchbox Twenty. We both loved this band and I knew this song like the back of my hand. Tears pricked my eyes at the meaning behind the song, and I struggled to hold them back.

Blade must have sensed this and he pulled me closer and gripped my hand tight. Amazingly, I made it all the way to J without crying, but when he stepped towards me and took my hand from Blade, the first tear fell and more followed.

J's gaze caressed me and he smiled before lifting a hand to my cheek and gently brushing the tears away. He moved so he could whisper in my ear, "I've got you now, babe."

I took a deep breath. My emotions were all over the place, but mostly I was happy.

"I know," I whispered back, and we proceeded to promise ourselves to each other.

★★★

I smiled at Nash as he stood to make a speech. He winked at me and raised his glass. Then he looked at J. "J didn't ask me to make a speech but the fucker did ask me to make sure Madison got to the wedding on time, so I'm gonna take it upon myself to give a speech anyway." He turned his attention back to me. "This wedding's taken a long fuckin' time to happen, sweet thing, but J finally got his shit together and I have to hand it to him; I can see how happy he's made you." Looking back at J, he said, "You and I have had our differences, brother, but I can finally see what Madison sees in you. Doesn't mean though, that I'm not watching out for her still. Keep her happy and we'll all be fuckin' happy." He paused and then broke out in a huge grin. "Here's to the happy couple; may they continue to piss each other off for the rest of their lives."

Nash sat back down and I couldn't help myself. Leaning over to J, I asked, "Why did you choose Nash to get me to the wedding?"

"You love him, and I love you. Plus, Nash knows how to handle you; knows how to calm you and I figured you might need that today." He grinned at me. "I'm trying to change my asshole ways, babe. Trying to get along with that fucker for you."

"Well you scored points today, J. Lots of points."

His eyes lit up. "What the fuck do those points get me? Cause I'm ready to cash them in right now."

I kissed him and then murmured, "That. Anything else, you're going to have to work for."

He smirked. "I think we've established that the last thing I need to work for is your pussy."

He was so right.

★★★

"Congratulations, honey," my mum said as she enveloped me in a hug.

"Thanks, Mum." She'd spent some time with me this morning helping me get ready but after that I hadn't seen much of her. This was one of the only things about today that I was disappointed in. That and the fact that my father was an asshole and not worth having at my wedding.

"Your father -" she started but I cut her off.

"Please don't mention him, Mum. Not today."

"Okay, honey," she said with a hint of sadness in her voice.

"Thank you."

"J's a lucky man," she murmured. "And I'm so happy that you found a man who loves you as much as he does."

I hugged her again. It meant a lot to me that one of my parents knew how good J was for me, and supported me in my choice.

As we broke our hug, I noticed J giving me the look that said 'get your ass over here'. "I've got to go and see what J wants, Mum, but I'll catch up with you a little later on, okay?"

She nodded and I made my way to my bossy biker. He looked hot today dressed in his jeans, tight black t-shirt and cut. It was pretty much his standard attire but I could tell he'd taken extra care today. And that body of his. My eyes soaked him in. His muscles flexed under that t-shirt and I was getting anxious to get it off of him.

He noticed me checking him out and smirked at me. "How long you reckon it would take to get you out of here and under me somewhere?"

I was just about to answer him when we were interrupted by some of his biker friends. He pulled me close and I whispered back, "Not long, baby, so let's hurry this along."

He looked down at me and shook his head. "You're gonna kill me one day, you know that, right?"

★★★

J draped his arm over the back of my chair and leant close to me. "You ready for our first dance, sweetheart?"

"Oh God, J, are you going to kill me with this song too?"

He grinned at me. "You liked that other one?"

"Yes," I murmured "I loved that you picked that. Who knew you could be so deep?"

"Fuck, babe. My cock gets hard when you say deep," he groaned.

I smacked him lightly on the arm. "Can you get your mind out of the gutter for even a moment?"

"Not when you're next to me. And not when I haven't fucked you for a good twenty four hours."

I decided it was time to play with him. I turned my head so our lips were close, and whispered, "I did what you said."

He looked perplexed. "And what was that?"

"You said not to wear any underwear."

His eyes widened. "Christ, woman. Don't fucking tell me that now." He looked away from me and then back at me before saying, "This dance is gonna have to wait." He grabbed my hand and abruptly stood up, pulling me with him.

However just as he did that, Griff, our MC for tonight, called out, "Time for your first dance, you lucky bastard."

I stifled a laugh; J actually looked pained. "Come on, baby. Let's get this done and then you can take me out of here and fuck me," I said just loudly enough for him to hear me.

Now he just looked pissed off. But he pulled me towards the dance floor. He wrapped his arms around me and rested his hands on my ass. Then he promised, "One dance and then I swear I'm gonna fuck you so you never forget it. You'll remember our first time as a married couple for the rest of your fucking life, Mrs Reilly."

I broke out in a huge smile. "I like the sound of that," I said.

He chuckled. "Yeah, so do I, babe."

I shook my head. "No, J. I meant that I liked you calling me Mrs Reilly."

His face softened, and he lightly kissed me. "Been a long time coming, sweetheart, but I finally made you mine."

The music started playing, and J nodded as I took in the words of the song he'd chosen. Tears threatened again as I listened to "(Everything I Do) I Do It For You" by Bryan Adams.

I curled my hand around his neck and pulled his face down to mine. "I was yours from the first day we met, J, you just didn't know it."

Epilogue

Jason

I SAT UP AND LOOKED AT MADISON. "YOU READY?"

"Yeah, move." She waved her hand indicating I should get out of the way.

I laughed, and stood up, and she took my place.

The tattooist smiled at her and then she got to work on Madison's tattoo, the one on her wrist that matched mine.

The tattooist enquired, "Is this your wedding date I'm adding to this tat?"

"Yes. Is it a dead giveaway that we're on our honeymoon?" Madison laughed.

"You do have that just married feel, yeah," the tattooist admitted, and then asked Madison, "How the hell did you get your husband to agree to ink himself with this tattoo? Mine wouldn't have a bar of it. He'd mutter something about sentimental bullshit and how he's not into that shit." She looked at me and winked.

"J actually got the tat before me; it's his design. And after knowing him for twelve years, I'm starting to realise that he's a sentimental bastard."

"No shit," the chick muttered, hitting me with a look of surprise.

Madison dug my grave marked 'pussy' even further by adding, "Oh, you should see my wedding ring that he had engraved. On the inside of the band is a replica of this tat with these dates on it too. His is the same."

"Fuck me," the tattooist said, shaking her head. Then she looked at me again and said, "For future reference, where do I find a guy like you? You know, just in case my husband runs off with some slut."

"Trust me, babe, you don't want a guy like me. I'm a moody fuck at the best of times, just ask my wife," I said.

"Good with his hands though," Madison teased, and they both laughed.

"Well, you can't argue with that. But this tat is something else; I love it when guys come in here getting symbolic stuff like this."

My phone rang and I excused myself, and walked outside.

"Griff. What's up?"

"Just sending through an email conversation I tracked down."

"Why are you sending it to me, brother?"

"It's between Marcus and the Adelaide President; a conversation about the pictures of you and that blonde that were taken when you were down there. They set you up on that one, J. Seems he paid the bitch to hit on you and make it look like you guys had hooked up."

"The fucking bitch was all over me that night; I couldn't get her off me."

"Marcus always planned to use it against you."

I fought the rising anger I felt towards Marcus; this anger never seemed to go away, and I wondered what would happen if the day came where I failed to contain it. "Thanks, Griff."

"Thought you might want to show it to Madison, in case she had any lingering doubt. You don't need to start your marriage off with that shit between you."

I saw what he was saying. Madison had surprised the shit out of me when she'd blindly accepted my word that nothing happened, and for me, it had been a real turning point for us. It proved to me just how much faith and trust she had in me.

We hung up and I headed back inside. Madison was just finishing up with the tattooist so I paid the bill, and then we headed outside into the sunshine. March in Port Douglas was beautiful and we'd had a great time over the last two weeks. Tomorrow we headed home; back to deal with this club shit. Until then, I'd enjoy having my wife to myself.

"Who was on the phone?" she asked.

"Griff."

"Is everything okay?"

I pulled my phone out and passed it to her, the message open and ready for her to read. "Yeah baby, he sent me this for you to read."

She frowned as she took the phone off me. A minute later she looked up at me, smiled and handed the phone back to me.

"So?" I asked her.

"J, I didn't need to read that to know you were being truthful about that woman."

"Really?"

"Really. We've been through a hell of a lot together, and I'm at a place now where I know you. I know that you love me. I know that this is forever, no matter what. And I know that I'm the only one for you. You've laid your soul out for me, baby, flaws and all; you've given me all of you." She rested her hand gently against my cheek. "You might be a dirty mouthed, moody asshole, but you love with all your heart and that's all a woman can ask for. So yeah, I don't need further proof of your love and commitment."

Fuck me.

I kissed her and then murmured, "I love you."

She leant her forehead against mine. "I love you, too."

We stayed connected like that for a couple of minutes, letting that settle in.

When we finally pulled apart, she smiled and promised me the world. "We're getting our forever, J."

THE END

.

Bonus Scenes

But wait, there's more!
I couldn't NOT give you this scene.

Nash
After the Wedding

FUCK ME, THIS CHICK WAS SOMETHING FUCKING ELSE. I'd be having words with Madison when I saw her next for not introducing me and Serena earlier. I stood transfixed as she kicked her heels off. Most chicks would just kick them off. Not this one. She wore sexy like a second skin. Her flirty eyes held mine as she seductively eased out of those fuck-me shoes. My cock stood up, screaming for some attention. Hell, who the fuck was I kidding? She'd had my cock hard all fucking night.

"Nash, how many chicks do you screw in an average week?"

What the fuck? What kind of chick asked that type of question? I answered her honestly. "As many as I can talk into it."

She gave me an impatient look. "Yeah, give me a number. Ball park."

I shrugged. Fuck, I hoped this didn't put an end to our fun tonight. "Seven on a good week. But average is probably three."

I waited for her to call it quits but was happy as fuck when she started taking off her dress.

"Thank Christ," she said, "I'm sick to death of dud lays. You sound like a man who knows what he's doing."

I grinned, and popped the button on my jeans. "Sweet thing, once I'm finished with you, you won't even fuckin' remember those dud lays. I'll wipe them from your memory. All you'll remember will be my cock and its many talents."

Her dress hit the floor and a minute later so did her bra and panties. I ripped off the remainder of my clothes and grabbed my cock, stroking it. Her gaze was fixed on it. "You gonna suck it, darlin'?" I asked.

She stepped towards me, and promised, "Oh, I'm going to suck it. It'll be my pleasure."

Christ. This chick was fucking hot; I was beginning to worry she'd have me shooting my load before the festivities really got going.

She moved my hand and took over the stroking of my dick. Her hands were fucking magical but I wanted that sweet mouth on me. "Babe, time to get down to it," I urged her.

She grinned. "You're a pushy bastard, aren't you?"

A moment later she was on her knees and my cock was enjoying the mad skills of her tongue and lips. She swirled and sucked her way to getting me off and when she began massaging my balls, I placed my hand on her head and groaned, "Darlin', unless you want my cum down your throat, you'd better get your lips off my dick."

She slowly eased me out of her mouth and gave my balls one last lick before she stood up. Her hand gripped my dick and stroked it. "You got a condom?" she asked.

I nodded at my jeans on the floor, and she let me go to grab it. My gaze travelled over her ass as she bent over. Shit, that was one fine ass. I'd bet my last dollar that she spent a lot of time working on that ass.

She came back to me with the condom out of its wrapper, and quickly got it in place. Standing on her toes, she whispered in my ear, "My pussy's so fucking wet for you, Nash. You ready to bang me and wipe my memory?"

Holy fuck! My lips smashed down onto hers and I kissed her like a mad man possessed. She was fucking into this and that was the biggest turn on for me. I walked her backwards to the bed and as the back of her legs hit the bed, I swiftly lifted her and threw her down on the bed. Her long blonde hair splayed out underneath her, and her eyes begged me to get down and fucking dirty. I took a minute though to bless my eyes with the sight of her glorious fucking tits. Serena had one of the best racks I'd ever fucking come across. The way she was lying on the bed, all revved up and ready to go, was a vision of pure sex. Hell, this was going to be a damn good fuck. Of that, I was sure.

She surprised me by sitting up and kneeling on the bed in front of me. "I'm on top," she said.

I raised my eyebrows. "Thought you wanted me to bang you, not the other way around?"

She smiled devilishly. "Yeah, that too. But first, we do it my way."

Fuck, I loved the sound of this. "We're going all night, aren't we darlin'?"

"I fucking hope so, biker boy. You've got a reputation to live up to; I want to still be screaming out your name tomorrow morning."

I didn't waste anymore time; a minute later I was under her and her wet pussy was making sweet promises to my cock.

She slowly lowered herself onto me but didn't let me very far in. Her hips swivelled and she circled the tip of my dick with wetness. Those lips of hers felt divine, and I tried to thrust a little. Smiling at me, she shook her head. "All in good time, baby," she said.

The maddening tease continued as she kept circling my cock

with her pussy, until finally she took my full length inside. Christ, she felt so good. I held her hips and we began to fuck. I let her control the pace and she went slow. Slow and deep. I kept my eyes glued to her tits; they were magnificent in the way they bounced, and I couldn't wait to get some speed up so they bounced a whole lot fucking more.

"Nash," she breathed," Your cock fucking rocks. Anyone ever told you that?"

"Yeah, babe. All the fucking time," I groaned. Serena had a dirty mouth to match mine and it was getting me off quick. "Now, you gonna let me fuck you or are you gonna keep fucking teasing me?"

"I'm ready for you to take over, biker boy. Show me what you've got."

I flipped her and wasted no time getting back inside of her. She wrapped her legs around me and held on tight while I screwed the fuck out of her. We fucked hard and fast, and were covered in sweat as we reached for our orgasms.

"Nash!" she screamed out my name, and her pussy clenched around me as she came. Her head fell back on the pillow and her eyes squeezed shut as she lost herself in the pleasure. I kept thrusting, the feel of her pussy amazing as it kept pulsing around me.

"Fuck!" I roared as the orgasm gripped me and I came.

I collapsed on top of her and she moved her arms so that her hands tangled in my hair. We stayed like that for awhile; both needing the time to recover from that fucking amazing orgasm.

Eventually she shifted, so I moved my head to look in her eyes. She was smiling at me.

I grinned back at her.

"The girls didn't lie to me when they said you were the one who could rock my world tonight," she said.

"Anytime you want your world rocked, you call on me, sweet thing. Cause you rocked my fucking world just as much."

"It's a shame you live so far away. I could do with a talented cock on call like yours."

I threw my head back and laughed. "You know how to turn a man on, baby. Give me a minute and then we can put my talents to use again," I said and winked at her.

Yeah, I'd be having strong fucking words with Madison when she got back from her honeymoon. It was a fucking crime keeping this chick from me.

Fierce Bonus Chapter

Harlow

Takes Place at the End of Fierce
- At Scott's Birthday Party

"SIT," I SAID TO MADISON AS I PATTED THE LOUNGE NEXT to me.

She smiled and sunk down into the lounge. "I'm so tired but it's only eleven and I know that J will want to stay awhile longer to help Scott celebrate his birthday."

Looking at her, I noticed that she looked exhausted. "Why are you so tired?"

She paused; it looked like she was weighing up what to say. Eventually she sighed and said, "J and I have been fighting. Well, not full on arguing, but let's just say that we have some issues to work through and I'm not sleeping well while we do that. Plus, I've been working some long hours at the shop lately."

I frowned. "I don't want to pry, mainly because we're still getting to know each other, but if you ever need someone to talk to, I'm here."

She reached for my hand and squeezed it. "Thanks, honey. I

really appreciate that."

"It's what friends are for," I said, giving her hand a squeeze back.

"Absolutely," she said, and gave me a huge smile. "I'm so glad that Scott found you. I never in a million years would have pictured him with a woman like you but I'm over the moon that he has you in his life. And not just for his sake; I'm glad because it means I've got you in my life too."

Her words sent warmth through me; I loved that she felt the same way about me that I felt about her. After my best friend had cheated on me with my boyfriend, I'd lost faith in friendships a little. Once trust has been broken in your life, you tend to find it hard to give it to others. Cassie was the first person I'd opened myself up to after it all happened. She'd taught me to trust again and Scott was also teaching me this. I had a feeling that Madison would be another new friend worthy of my faith in her.

We were interrupted by a sexy drawl we both knew well. "My two favourite ladies. Why are you sitting in the corner away from the party?"

I looked up to find Nash grinning at us. "We're just having some girly time while Scott and J are busy," I answered him as I flicked my eyes to where Scott was. Jealousy shot through me at the sight of a club whore throwing herself at him. I'd seen her around the clubhouse a lot lately; she appeared to have a strong interest in Scott. He was scowling at her and I could just imagine the nasty words he was saying to her. I had nothing to worry about; my man was clear that his only interest was in me. It didn't stop me being jealous though whenever a woman approached him.

Nash followed my gaze. "That bitch has no shot, Harlow."

He swung his face back to look at me and I was touched by what I saw there. For all his crudeness and sexy banter, Nash genuinely cared about mine and Scott's relationship. The look on his face currently told me that he wanted me to know that Scott was all mine.

I smiled at him. "I know," I murmured.

"Good," he said, "I'd hate a slut like her to come between you two."

"Shit," Madison muttered, and I turned to look at her.

"What?" I asked.

She didn't answer me straight away but rather stood up, a determined look on her face. I stood too and gave her a questioning look.

"J," was all she said as she jerked her head in the direction of Scott and J.

I directed my attention to them and sucked in a breath when I saw J stalking towards us. Shit, he didn't look happy.

"Nash you need to leave," Madison suggested quite forcefully.

Nash scowled. "If he's got a problem, sweet thing, he can -"

Madison cut him off. "Nash, why do you have to push it? Just leave, okay?"

I had no clue what was going on here but by the looks on their faces, something heavy was going down. Madison was throwing him a look that screamed 'get out of here now', while Nash was standing his ground and had firmly planted himself in the line of J's fire.

I jumped at J's voice when he finally reached us. "What the fuck, Nash?" he boomed.

Madison got in between them, trying to diffuse the situation. "J, just leave it, okay?"

Nash's face was a mask of anger and he cut in before J could reply, "No, fuck it, Madison. If he's got a problem, we can settle this once and for all now." I'd figured out over the past few weeks that J and Nash pushed each other's buttons. Nash looked ready to take J on.

"I do have a fucking problem, motherfucker. I go away for a couple of months and I get back to find that you've been trying to talk your way into my woman's pants." J thundered.

Nash snarled and stepped forward to get in J's face. "You don't know me very well, J, if you think I'd fuck another man's woman. I wasn't trying to get in her pants but I was trying to make sure she knew what she was doing by letting you into them, asshole."

"I think I know you very fucking well, Nash. You'd fuck anything, and I'm betting that would include another man's woman. You need to back the fuck off Madison because she's mine, and I don't take too fucking kindly to other men stepping in."

Shit, J was one territorial male. I hadn't seen him in action before; he didn't muck around.

"Oh, for fuck's sake, J. I've told you, Nash wasn't trying to get in my pants," Madison stepped into the argument. She had a wild look about her and J scowled at her.

"Stay out of it, Madison. This is between me and Nash," he fumed, dismissing her with an angry glare.

She threw her hands up in the air. "Fine, I'm out. You two can sort this out between yourselves. I'm going home." She gave me an apologetic look before turning and stalking out of the room.

I was standing in stunned silence until Scott made his way over to us. He was pissed off; I knew his moods fairly well by now and I knew there were no crinkled eyes to be found tonight. This put me in a pissed off mood too; it was Scott's birthday and damn it, I wanted crinkles tonight. If J and Nash kept this up, they just might have me to contend with.

"You two need to get your shit together," Scott said in that voice of his that meant business.

Both J and Nash glared at him; it was like a stand off of bossy men, none willing to back down.

I waited to hear who would cave first but none of them did. Oh, good God, these men! I stepped forward and caught all of their attention. "J, have you any idea how much Madison missed you while you were gone? I made her coffee nearly every day and listened to her moan about you being gone. It looks to me like you're wasting precious time here. You've got a woman ready and waiting to make all your dreams come true and here you are, waving your dick at Nash, who, can I just say, has no interest in Madison. I have no idea what your beef is with him but I can tell you, women get tired of men who beat their chest repeatedly, so I'd suggest you forget it and just go home and let Madison love you." I turned my attention to Nash and shook my head at him. "Nash, for God's sake, move on. Arguing with J is pointless. Don't you have a chick to bang somewhere?" I finished and waited for their response. All three of them were looking at me with raised eyebrows and stunned looks on their faces.

Oops, maybe I'd overstepped. Shit, Scott would be mad at me and that was the last thing I wanted on his birthday. I held up my hands in a defensive gesture. "Okay, just ignore me. As you were," I muttered and leant down to pick up my bag. If they were all going to be mad at me, I was leaving. I slung my bag over my should and took a step to leave.

Scott reached out and curled his arm around my waist and pulled me to him. "Where you going, babe?" he asked, his face close to mine and his eyes searching mine. Butterflies hit my stomach; Scott had a way of making me feel like the only person in the world sometimes and this was one of those times. In the midst of this argument, he'd managed to block everyone else out and give me his full attention. No other man had ever done that for me.

"I think I've probably said too much and involved myself in something I shouldn't have, so it's best if I leave you boys to it," I admitted quietly. The feel of Scott's arm around my waist, his warm breath on my skin, and his intense gaze were muddling my thoughts.

"Let's get something straight here; if you've got something to say, you say it. You don't hold back. Can't say I'll always agree with it but I always want to hear what you're thinking. Okay?"

I nodded. "Yes," I murmured in agreement.

He held me close for a moment longer and held my eyes before nodding once and letting me go. Then he turned to J and Nash. "I think Harlow's pretty much covered it. I'm going home but I want you two to sort through your shit once and for all. We've got too much other stuff going on at the moment; we don't need to add your grievances to it," he muttered before grabbing my hand and leading me out of the room.

★★★

Scott unlocked his front door and stood back as he gestured for me to go inside. I smiled at him and his lips curled up in a small grin in return. Crinkles. Oh, my. I lived for those crinkles.

"What?" he asked, and I realised that I was rooted to the spot while I stared at his eyes.

I shook my head. "Nothing." I quickly moved past him and entered his house. He followed closely behind and the anticipation of what he had planned for tonight set my nerves alight with excitement. After Bullet had almost raped me, we'd stopped having sex for a little while but finally we were back where we'd left off. Sex with Scott was the best I'd ever had and I refused to let Bullet come between us.

At the end of the hall, I turned and headed towards his bedroom. I kicked my shoes off as I went and then lifted my dress over my head and left it on the floor as I continued to walk. Scott sucked in a breath and the sound was music to my ears. I reached behind me and undid my bra, letting it fall to the ground too. As I hooked my fingers into the top of my panties and began to lower them, his hands landed on mine and stopped me. I felt him as he moved closer behind me.

"Babe, you've gotta leave something for me to take off," he said gruffly.

I smiled at the desire that was clear in his voice. Scott's need for me wasn't something he hid and I loved this; it turned me on even more.

Impulsively, I turned around and wrapped my arms around his

neck. His hands slid around my ass and he lifted me up so that my legs wrapped around him. Scott was strong and he easily continued our journey to his bedroom as he carried me.

"Is this my birthday present?" he asked with a teasing glint in his eyes.

"What, the cake wasn't enough?" I teased back.

"No, babe, I want more. I'll never have enough when it comes to you."

My mouth came down onto his in a demanding kiss. I'd never have enough of him either. He kissed me back, sending me wild. Sweet Jesus, this man was good with his tongue. Eventually he pulled away and let me down because we'd found our way to his bedroom. I stood in front of him in silence as he swept his gaze over my body. My nipples hardened and my panties almost melted off from the heat he was sending my way.

I dropped my eyes down to his jeans and took in his hard cock. He followed my eyes. "See what you do to me, baby?" he said, sex dripping from his words.

I nodded and reached out to undo his jeans but he flicked his hand out and stopped me. "Turn around," he growled.

Smiling to myself, I did what he said. He stepped right behind me, his erection pressing into me, and his breath warm on my neck. His hand snaked around my waist and his hand dipped down until he reached into my panties and stroked my clit with his thumb. I was so wet for him and he grunted in appreciation. His other hand wrapped around me and reached up to massage my breast.

"Baby, you make a man very happy. You're my birthday present," he murmured in his growly voice that never failed to hit my sweet spot.

The butterflies whooshed through me at his words. I leant my head back on his shoulder and sucked in a breath when he licked and sucked along my jaw. His thumb was working its magic on my clit and when he pushed two fingers inside, I shuddered in pleasure.

"Feels good, yeah?" he asked softly in between the kisses he was trailing along my neck.

"Yes," I moaned, unable to get any other words out. The pleasure was building in me and the waves were overtaking me. Every nerve ending was on fire with desire and pleasure and I almost couldn't form a thought in my head as I let it take over me.

"Good, because this is what you do to me too. When you touch me, Harlow, it's like I've never been fuckin' touched before in my life."

That was it for me. His words set a final wave of pleasure off and I finally succumbed and went with it. As the orgasm took hold, I shut my eyes and let it consume me. I let Scott consume me; body and soul. No man had ever had the power over me that he did; not the power to give me so much pleasure, nor the power to own my heart the way he did.

Acknowledgements

Usually I thank my family and friends first. This time around, I truly need to thank my book world people first because they are the ones who helped me so much with Blaze. Family, you know I love you always but bear with me while I thank the people who have helped me get my books out there.

To my #STORMCHASERS - again, you ladies ROCK! You girls are my book family and I owe so much to you. The support and encouragement you offer is out of this world and there are not enough words to properly thank you.

Melanie Sassymum - you blow me away, lady! You are one of the most selfless, kind, caring and giving people I have ever met. You do so much for authors all over the world and I am one of the luckiest because I get to call you friend too. You really do go above and beyond. I will never be able to thank you enough. Can't wait to get on the dance floor with you chick and celebrate our friendship!

Elle Raven - FARK!! I feel ya! I'm not sure if I've ever met someone and bonded instantly like I did with you. You are fucking crazy, awesome, hilarious and sweet heavens above, I can't wait to hang out with you again! Thank you for all your support and your friendship.

Jani Kay - my soul sister - I don't even know where to start... I feel like I've known you forever. And I can't imagine a life without you in it now. Thank goodness for Skype and Facebook, huh?! Thank you for helping me find my way in this book world, and for all your faith in me and support of me. I am SO looking forward to the shit we're going to get up to ;)

Louisa - love you, girl!!! Thank you for your belief in me and for making me kick ass covers! You give so much - one day I'll get you back! And you can give me that stern look all you like; I won't be paying any attention to it ;)

Nadine - thank you for still loving me after I shocked you. You are an amazing friend! I actually can't believe that we've never met in person because it feels like we have. Thank you for all your support and love xx

Bloggers - you ladies are a special kind of awesome!! Thank you for sharing my books, news, teasers etc. I owe so very much to you all. xx

Lilliana Anderson, Lili St Germain, Rachel Brookes - you ladies are awesome!! Thank you so very much for sharing my stuff all the time and for offering me support like no other xx

Eliahn - k bae - LOVE YOU chick!! One day I will write a book for you to read, my darling.

Kathleen - When the fuck are you taking me out for that drink, woman?? OH wait, I'M taking you out! *smacks head* I owe you so very much. You love me unconditionally and I'd be lost without you, dude. Thank you, thank you, thank you!! And don't be mad at me for not thanking you first! You know you're my #1

To the rest of my family - thank you for listening to me rave on and on and on and on and on about books ;) I love you all xx

About the Author

Nina Levine is an Aussie writer who writes stories about hot, alpha men and the tough, independent women they love.

When she isn't creating with words, she loves to create with paint and paper. Often though, she can be found curled up with a good book and some chocolate.

Signup for my newsletter: http://eepurl.com/OvJzX

I will be releasing a FREE serial to subscribers of my newsletter. Roxie's story is COMING SOON!

I love to chat with the readers of my book so please visit me or contact me here:

Website: http://ninalevinebooks.blogspot.com.au
Facebook: https://www.facebook.com/AuthorNinaLevine
Twitter: https://twitter.com/NinaLWriter
Pinterest: http://www.pinterest.com/ninalevine92/
(check out my boards full of the pictures that inspired me while writing Storm)

I would also love it if you would consider leaving a review for Blaze on the site you bought it.

Reviews mean so very much to me xx

Blaze Playlist

I create playlists for all my books. Music inspires my stories and I almost always listen to it while writing. Here are the songs that helped inspire Blaze:

All of Me by John Legend
Don't Kill The Magic by Magic!
Heaven by Bryan Adams
How Do I Live by Trisha Yearwood
Hurts So Good by John Mellencamp
I Will by Matchbox Twenty
(Everything I Do) I Do It For You by Bryan Adams
Just Give Me A Reason by Pink & Nate Ruess
Love Runs Out by OneRepublic
Magic by Coldplay
Medicine by Shakira & Blake Shelton
One More Night by Maroon 5
She's In Love With The Boy by Trisha Yearwood
Shut Out The Lights by Keith Urban
The Story of Us by Taylor Swift
The Truth About Love by Pink
When You're Gone by Bryan Adams & Melanie C
Wild Wild Love by Pitbull & G.R.L.
You're Still The One by Shania Twain

Nash's Story

REVIVE (Storm MC #3)
by Nina Levine
Release Date: 21st July 2014

He doesn't do relationships. Neither does she. But they can't fight the attraction any longer...

Nash Walker hides the demons that consume his soul. He buries them deep and distracts himself with sex. Anything to avoid facing a past full of heartbreak and regret; anything to numb the pain that he struggles with daily.

Velvet Carr has spent years fighting her demons. It's a fight she's winning. That is, until Nash crashes his way into her life and into her heart.

It started out as a bit of harmless fun between friends; it wasn't meant to get complicated for either of them. But when two broken souls come together and arouse unwanted feelings in each other, complicated is what happens.

Can Nash and Velvet help heal each other and revive the love in their lives that they've both been refusing to allow in for years? Or will they let their demons ruin any chance they may have at happiness?